MW01531688

SONGS OF THE RAINBOW

MAUI ISLAND SERIES BOOK 7

KELLIE COATES GILBERT

AMG

PRAISE FOR KELLIE COATES GILBERT'S NOVELS

"If you're looking for a new author to read, you can't go wrong with Kellie Coates Gilbert." ~**Lisa Wingate**, NY Times best-selling author of *Before We Were Yours*

"Well-drawn, sympathetic characters and graceful language". ~**Library Journal**

"Deft, crisp storytelling" ~**RT Book Reviews**

"I devoured the book in one sitting." ~**Chick Lit Central**

"Gilbert's heartfelt fiction is always a pleasure to read." ~**Buzzing About Books**

"Kellie Coates Gilbert delivers emotionally gripping plots and authentic characters." ~**Life Is Story**

"I laughed, I cried, I wanted to throw my book against the wall, but I couldn't quit reading." ~**Amazon reader**

"I have read other books I had a hard time putting down, but this story totally captivated me." ~**Goodreads reader**

"I became somewhat depressed when the story actually ended. I wanted more." ~**Barnes and Noble reader**

ALSO BY KELLIE COATES GILBERT

Otherwise Engaged

All Fore Love

-

TEXAS GOLD SERIES

A Woman of Fortune

Where Rivers Part

A Reason to Stay

What Matters Most

-

STAND ALONE NOVELS

Mother of Pearl

* * *

Available at all retailers

www.kelliecoatesgilbert.com

SONGS OF THE RAINBOW

MAUI ISLAND SERIES, BOOK 7

Kellie Coates Gilbert

1

Christel and Evan pulled their car into the main yard at Pali Maui and cut the engine. "Do you know what's up with this family meeting your mom called?" Evan asked.

Christel shook her head. "None whatsoever. She only said it was important that we all be here."

Her siblings often gathered at their mom's house. Especially since they all lived nearby—yet it wasn't like her mother to be this secretive.

Christel climbed from the vehicle and waved to Katie and Jon, who were walking toward them from the direction of their house. Willa followed her parents while carrying her little sister, Noelle. "Down. Down. Me want down," Noelle said, wiggling to get out of her sister's arms.

"Fine." Willa sighed with exasperation and lifted the toddler to the ground. Noelle immediately chased after their Cavapoo puppy named Givey.

"Hang onto her," Katie warned.

Willa rolled her eyes. "Of course." She took the little girl's hand. "I live to be Noelle's babysitter."

The comment drew a stern look from her father, who carried a sizeable aluminum pan covered with foil.

Two more cars slowly made their way up the long drive. One belonged to Christel and Katie's youngest brother, Shane, and the other to Aiden, the oldest of the two Briscoe boys. They both pulled to a stop and got out as Ava appeared and stood at her front door. She wiped her hands on a kitchen towel. "Good. You're all here. Come inside. I have a surprise."

The Briscoe siblings glanced at each other and headed for Ava's front door, stopping to kiss Ava's cheek as they entered.

Inside, Jon placed the pan on the counter. "Willa made us dinner. Her first attempt at seafood lasagna. She has a real future as a chef," he bragged.

Willa waved off his praise. "Don't go getting all fussy about this until you taste it. Like Dad said, it's my first try."

Ava looked at her granddaughter full-on with a wide smile. "I'm sure the dish will be delicious."

Aiden gave his mother a side hug. "So, what's this little gathering all about, Mom?"

Ava clasped her hands, barely hiding her enthusiasm for what she was about to say. "Well, Alani reached out to me this morning. As you know, Ori has hopes of expanding Ka Hale A Ke Ola. The resource center has been overflowing with people needing a place to sleep and a warm meal since the big storm. Islanders were hit hard and are finding it difficult to recover. As Ori explained to his mother and me, expansion takes resources...monetary resources. So, we all put our heads together and devised a plan."

"That sounds dangerous," Shane teased. He glanced down at the floor, turning his attention to his baby boy. "Don't eat that!" He quickly bent and pulled Givey's tail from his son's mouth. The baby toddler looked up and grinned, with dog hair plastered to his drooling mouth. "Ugh," Shane said as he bent to wipe his son's mouth clean. "Carson is at the stage where everything goes in his mouth."

Ava reached and pulled her grandson into her arms and hugged him tightly. "Babies do that." She turned to her family and smiled. "Back to Ori and our plan. I gathered you all here to bribe you."

"Bribe?" Katie asked.

"Yes." Ava paused as if considering how to put forth her proposal. Finally, she just said what was on her mind. "We're holding a big talent show and selling fundraising tickets. We'll also secure corporate sponsorships. We're all going to participate."

Christel turned her attention to her mom's boyfriend. "Tom, why do mothers do that? They tell you what they want as if it's a done deal. No question."

"You're asking me?" he said, laughing. "Have you met my mom?"

She hadn't, but the few things her mother had shared after her trip to Boston had hinted that Tom Strobe's mother was the queen of control freaks.

"So, this is the deal," Ava's face brightened. Using her one free hand, she passed out papers to everyone. "Here's the list. Christel, you and Evan are going to do a humorous skit. Katie, you and Jon are doing a dance number. Aiden..."

Before she could continue, both her sons held up open palms in protest. "Oh, no. We're not dancing or singing," they said in unison.

"Absolutely not," Aiden added for emphasis.

Ignoring them, Ava set Carson back down on the floor. "I have you two lip-syncing an old Carole King song...one of my favorites." She closed her eyes and swayed as she sang out. "*I feel the earth move under my feet.*"

"Oh, man," Aiden said, folding to his mother's wishes, as he often did. "You're going to owe us big time."

That earned a shoulder slap from Shane. "Hey, way to leave me hanging here, bro." He groaned as he surveyed his family's pleading faces.

"This is for Ori," Katie reminded as she looked down the list. "And all the people who use the services at the center."

"Yeah." Willa moved to the refrigerator and got herself a can of soda. "People like Halia and Kina." Her best friend and her mom used to live at the center. They'd met when Willa helped Ori out on a workday.

Halia and her daughter, Kina, now lived with three other women in a loft above a boutique in Pā'ia. One of the women inherited a plot of land nearby, and together, the roommates started a day retreat for women. They called it Banana Patch, partly because of the banana palms on the property and partly after a commune by that name here on Maui that folded years ago.

Halia and Kina were only one of many success stories showing how important Ori's efforts were.

"Okay, okay," Shane said, also folding under pressure to be magnanimous. "I'm in."

"We'll support you in whatever way we can, Mom," Aiden added.

Ava pulled her two sons into a shoulder hug. "That's my boys."

Aiden's phone buzzed. He pulled it from his pocket and answered, "Yeah. Captain Briscoe here."

Everyone immediately went silent, knowing a call from Maui Emergency Services could mean a rescue was necessary. They all waited and listened as Aiden nodded. "Yeah? No kidding?" He ran his hand through the top of his hair. "I'll be right there."

He clicked off.

"What is it?" Katie asked, immediately turning worried.

Ava frowned. "Son? Everything okay?"

Aiden pocketed his phone. "Yeah. I guess. I mean, someone just abandoned a baby at the station."

Evan frowned. "A baby?"

"Yeah. A tiny little girl. Left her in a box on the steps of the station."

2

Evan accompanied Aiden to the station in the event the situation required a doctor. It was rare that someone would take steps to bring an infant to an emergency station if they intended to harm the baby, but there was no telling what people were capable of.

"Man, I've heard of this happening, but we sure haven't faced this situation at the station before," Aiden said, gunning the engine a little past the speed limit.

Evan let out a sigh. "Yeah, it's unfortunate. Yet, I'm always grateful someone cares enough to ensure the baby is safe and out of harm's way. I've seen some situations go in the opposite direction."

Aiden and Evan sat silent, both highly aware of what medical professionals regularly see.

Aiden was thankful to have his brother-in-law by his side on this one. While Evan specialized in orthopedic surgery, he had completed a double residency at Baylor in Dallas, Texas, that included pediatric and adolescent medicine. He'd likely seen his share of abuse and abandonment cases during those years. He'd know what protocols to follow, even if Aiden didn't.

They arrived minutes later to find Jeremy Hogan standing in the open doorway. He frantically waved them inside.

Aiden patted him on the back as he moved into the station and glanced around. "What've we got?"

Jud Fogleman rushed to his side. "In the kitchen." He shook his head. "I can't believe someone wouldn't want their baby and just left it in a box."

Based on some of what Evan had told him on the way here, few parents who left their baby at a station were evil. Often desperation drove them to the only decision they found viable.

Aiden waved for Evan to follow as he broke into a jog. He passed the emergency vehicles, crossed the apparatus room, and headed toward the kitchen.

The small room was crowded, with guys checking out the situation. Aiden pushed his way through until he spotted Meghan sitting at the table, holding a bundle in her arms. She looked up at him, her blue eyes brimming with emotion.

The sight caught him off guard and caused him to halt immediately.

This was a new Meghan—someone he'd never noticed before. She almost looked...well, vulnerable.

She lifted her arm, revealing her signature tiger tattoo. The feline's snarling teeth portrayed a stunning contrast to the tender way Meghan pulled back the dirty blanket to reveal a tiny round head covered in downy hair.

Their eyes met, and Aiden felt himself unable to breathe.

She scowled. "What are you looking at?"

Aiden finally sucked in a ragged breath. "Uh, nothing." He reluctantly turned his attention to Evan, who cleared the way so he could get a closer look.

Evan reached for the infant. "May I?"

Meghan nodded and lifted the baby into Evan's arms. "She seems to be okay. We checked her vitals, and there are no marks on her anywhere," she reported.

A baby's cry rang out from across the room.

Aiden scowled and whipped around. "What's that?"

Meghan stepped back after leaving the tiny baby girl in Evan's care. "The other one."

"The other one?" Aiden and Evan asked simultaneously.

Jeremy raked his hands through the top of his hair. "Did I forget to tell you? There are two."

3

Christel pushed the lasagna around on her plate with her fork, still reeling from the text she'd received from Evan as they headed for the hospital with the babies.

Yes...babies. There were two of them. Someone had dumped two infants—a boy and a tiny girl—at the station. Unwanted children.

The notion was hard to fathom, given her craving to be a mother. How many months had passed with her staring at a negative pregnancy test? How many times had tears sprouted and her gut had turned in on itself with disappointment when no bright line appeared?

It wasn't fair!

"Don't you like my lasagna, Aunt Christel?"

Christel glanced up into her waiting niece's face. "Oh, no... it's good. I'm not hungry. That's all."

She caught her mother's eyes, then quickly looked away. Despite her best effort to hide her feelings, her mom cornered her in the kitchen after the meal.

"Honey, are you okay?"

"I'm fine," she lied.

She felt the familiar touch of her mother's fingers against her bare arm. Those fingers sent a message that did not need to be spoken. Her mom knew the pain she was feeling and ached for her.

Her mom squeezed her arm before turning to the others. "Okay, let's get a pen and paper and finalize our plans for the fundraiser.

What followed was typical of her family...laughter, teasing, and plenty of jokes. The Briscoes were not afraid to make fun of one another, all in good fun, of course.

"You call that dancing?" Shane challenged as Katie proceeded to step all over Jon's feet when they attempted jitter-bugging.

Having had enough of her parents' antics, Willa finally stood and forced them to stop. "Okay, that's so lame." She turned. "No offense, Grammy Ava, but they need to do something like on TikTok."

"TikTok?" Tom asked.

"Yeah...hashtag dance moves." To show what she was talking about, she pulled out her phone, opened the popular video app, and scrolled through a series of three-minute videos depicting people dancing to the Brooks and Dunn song "*Neon Moon.*"

Jon leaned over and studied the video. "Yeah, we could do that."

Katie lifted her shoulders and shrugged. "Okay. I guess we could try."

Over the next half hour, the Briscoes circled Jon and Katie as they followed their daughter's tutoring.

"Like this?" Katie asked, lifting her arm in the air.

"Yeah, but bring it down slowly," Willa instructed. "And move your hips, Mom. You look like a statue."

Shane busted out laughing. "Yeah, move it...Miss Liberty."

That earned him a glare from his sister. "I'd like to see you try it," she quickly countered.

Not to be put off by a challenge, Shane popped up from the sofa. He motioned for Willa to join him, and together they moved their bodies in perfect synchronized motion. First, one of their arms went in the air and slowly lowered, following the curve of their bodies. Then, the second arm. Next, they twirled their bodies in a circle stirring their hips as if whipping up cake batter.

Christel had to admit her brother and niece were pretty good at this dance move.

In frustration, Katie waved them off. "Okay, okay. We get it."

"Don't worry, Mom. You and Dad can practice a lot before the big fundraiser." Her confidence did little to erase the irritation on Katie's face.

Tom stood and held out his hand to Ava. "C'mon, Grammy Ava. Let's show them how it's done." He beamed as she complied with his wishes and moved to place her hand in his own. He pulled her tightly against him and let his head rest on her hair as he guided her in a slow and intimate dance to the same tune.

Christel couldn't help but warm inside at the look on her mother's face. She'd met someone she adored, and it showed.

In fact, her mother was gloriously happy...even after all she'd been through.

It was then that her mom's often repeated counsel rang out in her mind. "It hurts when God says no to our dreams. Sometimes, His no leads to a better yes. Remember that, sweetheart."

Her mother had earned the right to make this claim. Not only had she lost her mother at an early age, but she'd suffered the loss of her husband, Christel's dad, to a tragic car accident. Worse, she'd later learned he had betrayed her with her best friend's daughter...a girl she loved like her own.

Despite all that, Ava had not only forgiven, but she'd

embraced the idea that joy came from within. She was determined to fill her life with happiness and purpose.

Christel longed to do the same.

She had, in fact, forgiven Mia. While they would never have the close relationship they'd once enjoyed, at least Christel no longer hated her for what she'd done.

She only wished she could be magnanimous with a baby in her arms.

After three raucous rounds of the card game, *Uno*—Christel was in the kitchen with Katie and Willa, cleaning up the last of the dinner mess, when she heard an engine outside. She moved to the kitchen window and looked out. "Looks like Aiden and Evan are home."

Katie pushed down the trash and bundled the bag into her hands before handing it off to Jon. "Take this out, will you?"

He planted a kiss on her forehead. "Anything for my dance queen." His eyes sparkled with laughter as he headed for the back door.

Katie looked at Christel. "You know, I'm not that bad."

Christel held back laughter. "No, Katie. You're really good." She choked a little on purpose.

Katie groaned out loud. "What is it with you people? I'm good."

Shane appeared and held up open palms. "No one's arguing, sis. You dance your heart out. I'm sure no one will laugh." He winked at Willa.

In the living area, the door opened, and in strode Evan, followed by Aiden. Both of them carried something in their arms.

Shane rubbed at his chin and moved to join his brother. "Dude, what is that?"

"It's a baby," Aiden reported.

"Two babies," Evan added.

"Two?" Ava exchanged glances with Tom before leaving her

spot on the sofa to join them at the door. "What do you mean two? Someone left twins?"

Evan nodded. "It appears that way. The good news is that we took them to the hospital, and they checked out just fine. These little ones are healthy."

Christel scowled and wiped her hand on a kitchen towel. "What are you doing with them?" It was a stupid question. Anyone with half a brain could figure out the answer to her question. The infants needed to be cared for. A better question was why Evan and Aiden were in that role.

She escaped having to pose that question when Willa leaned in to get a better look. "But why do you guys have them?"

Evan raised his gaze to Christel. "Because they needed someone to take care of them."

Her niece pulled back a blanket to reveal a tiny face. "Forever?"

"Temporarily," Aiden told them. "The social worker met us at the hospital. As a doctor, Evan was approved to take custody until the authorities could make other arrangements. The courts will want to weigh in. Studies will have to be done. She says the process in situations like these can be pretty arduous."

"The best interests of the children remain paramount in every decision." He again let his gaze drift to Christel. "For now, what is best is for someone to care for them until a permanent situation can be decided upon. I thought..."

"No!" Christel nearly screamed, interrupting him.

"What?"

She shook her head violently. "I said no. If you think I'm going to take two abandoned infants home with me only to have to give them up later...." She lifted her chin. "No."

She threw a look at her husband. Was he out of his mind?

Evan was nonplussed at her outrage. He moved slowly toward her.

Tears formed as he neared.

Christel felt her insides shake as Evan leaned and kissed the top of her head. She dared a glance down at the baby in his arms. The tiny infant opened its eyes and peered directly into her own.

It was at that moment that she lost her ability to say no.

She lost control of her heart.

4

After things wrapped up at his mom's house, Aiden made a quick decision to return to the station, convincing himself he only wanted to check on things. Crew members would reach out to him should an emergency arise that needed his attention, even in the middle of the night. Many nights passed with nothing more than his team members sitting around playing cards. Even so, Aiden was drawn back to the station on this particular evening.

He could argue the reason, but the voices inside his head had been screaming her name all night. He knew going down this path was dangerous. Meghan McCord was a co-worker, a subordinate...which meant she was off-limits.

Aiden couldn't remember the last time he felt something—anything—for a woman. His focus remained directed on his career...and its pitfalls. Dire emergencies and making split-second decisions could mean life or death. Like it or not, they took their toll.

If he had to admit it, and he rarely did, the past year had not been easy.

He'd been secretly wrestling the demons of being the emergency worker who responded to a fatal accident on the Road to Hana—the crash that had taken his dad's life. With no warning, he discovered his dad was not the man he'd always looked up to. His father had made destructive decisions that hurt his entire family.

Aiden was just feeling steady again when he was in the boat explosion. The months that followed held pain and extreme dedication in order to rehabilitate.

As he healed and could return to duty, he found himself consumed in transitioning into the role of captain and dedicating himself to being the best leader he could be.

His plate had been full, both physically and emotionally. Even if he'd been attracted to someone of the female persuasion, he had little time to pull away from his focus.

Things of the heart never seemed to wait for a good time.

Aiden let his mind wander to that fake kiss, the one that kept coming to mind without invitation.

Nothing he had said or done seemed to thwart that girl Shane set him up with. She was definitely wacko and wouldn't move off her determination to win him over. Nothing he said convinced her to accept that he was not interested. That is until Meghan planted a deep and highly romantic kiss on his lips and claimed he was already taken.

Aiden laughed to himself. That sure did the trick. He hadn't seen Sydney since.

Meghan McCord was extraordinarily talented at her job, tough, and gutsy. She was fearless in rescue situations, often putting herself in harm's way to save another. She ran faster, swam farther, and climbed higher than most of her male counterparts. It seemed no one had let her in on the fact that she was far less bulky and muscled. Can't wasn't in her vocabulary.

No one messed with Meghan and escaped the encounter unscathed...not even the guy who had become abusive. With the help of her friends, including Aiden, she'd ultimately sent the dude packing, wishing he'd chosen someone else to dump his ugly on.

Aiden now realized there was a softer side to his tough co-worker.

Meghan looked good with an infant in her arms. Tender and nurturing were not characteristics he'd ever associated with her. Yet, there was no mistaking how she held that baby and looked into the tiny girl's face. No matter the message that fierce tiger tattoo on her arm sent, it appeared Meghan was far more tenderhearted than he'd credited her for.

Aiden pulled into the station and parked next to Meghan's car.

He glanced in the rearview mirror, smoothed his hair, then popped a breath mint and tossed the remainder of the roll onto his passenger seat. A sense of anticipation filled him as he took a deep breath and climbed from his SUV.

The star-filled sky was alive with raw energy. He could feel them vibrating somehow, whispering in a way the ears could not hear—hinting at possibility and expectation.

He climbed the steps leading to the entrance two at a time and reached for the station door. Before he could open it, a feminine voice broke through the darkness. "Hey."

Startled, Aiden turned.

Only a few feet away, Meghan sat on the ground, cross-legged. Despite the dim light, Aiden could see her long hair cascading over her shoulder.

His eyebrows lifted. "What are you doing out here?"

She leaned back and reclined with her head nested against her folded arms, the grass against her back. "Aren't they beautiful?"

Aiden followed her gaze. "The stars?"

"When I was little," she said, continuing her focus on the sky, "I used to try to count them."

His face broke into a smile. "Any luck?"

"With counting them?" she asked. "Not really. I enjoyed the process, the focus it required...the possibilities," she said, letting her voice drift. She patted the space beside her.

Aiden hung back. While flattered at the invitation, he knew how it would look if the guys saw him out here lying on the ground peering into the dark sky.

"Lighten up, cowboy."

The comment pinched. He shrugged off his hesitation, folded beside her, and looked up into the sky. "Are you trying to count them now?"

"Nah...I'm old enough now to know you can't possibly number the stars in the sky. I like that about them. The little diggers are too vast, too numerous to quantify. No, I was scoping out Scorpius."

"Scorpius?"

"Scorpius is one of the sky's most conspicuous and recognizable constellations, known as the fish hook. Hawaiians call it *Manaiakalani* after the magical fishing line they believe in having been used to haul the islands out of the sea."

He grinned, intensely aware that she smelled a lot like the gardenias in his mom's yard. "Okay, yeah. I know what Scorpius is. I'm a little surprised to find you are so interested in all that."

"Are you kidding? Who wouldn't be interested in such a vast system, so expansive, so massive...there seems to be no end." She sat up, and her voice grew excited. "For example, take the Vela Pulsar. Did you know that particular supernova travels more than twelve hundred kilometers per second? And, were you aware that the Vela emits a radio frequency that sounds like a song?"

Aiden turned to face her. "You don't say."

"It's true. Look it up! Check out Louie Giglio's videos on YouTube."

"Oh, I'm not questioning the veracity of your claim. I'm only surprised that you dig this stuff." There was a lot he didn't know about Meghan, things he thought he might like to learn.

She laid back again and pointed into the sky. "I find it comforting to know there is something so much bigger out there. Something that intricate didn't just happen."

He was glad it was dark, and she couldn't see him raise his eyebrows. "You believe in a Creator?"

Meghan sighed. "Of course. Don't you?"

"Well, yeah. I just didn't know..."

She playfully slapped his belly with the back of her hand. "Seems there's a lot you don't know, Captain."

"Aiden."

"Huh?"

"We're not officially on the clock. You can call me Aiden."

A moment of silence ticked by before she sat up and looked over at him. "So, Aiden...where'd you take those babies?"

"Dr. Matisse and my sister took them home. At least for now. My sister has been unable to conceive. At first, she was reluctant, knowing the situation was temporary. My brother-in-law convinced her caring for the tiny twins was the right thing to do."

He watched her silhouette as she slowly nodded. "Good. That's good."

"Yeah, don't get me wrong...I'm glad the mother chose to leave them somewhere safe and unharmed, but who leaves their babies on a doorstep? Why?"

"Lots of reasons, I suppose," Meghan said wistfully. "Not everyone is cut out to parent a baby—or two. Especially if the person faces hard things, like a lack of financial resources or support from the father. Maybe they don't like kids."

"Who doesn't like kids?"

"Lots of people."

Again, silence.

Aiden sensed she was not revealing something. He hesitated, not wanting to intrude. Curiosity got the better of him. "Meghan?"

"Yeah?" She folded her arms over her knees and dropped her gaze to the ground. "Okay, what are you wanting to know?"

He felt caught. "Uh, nothing. I mean, nothing you don't want to tell me."

She shrugged. "I'm not hiding anything. It's no secret I was a foster kid."

The news hit him hard. "Oh."

"Yeah, I don't take out ads. But I'm not ashamed of the fact. It is what it is. I was one of the lucky ones, given the circumstances. My mom died before I could even know her. My dad... well, he wasn't a good man. The authorities stepped in when I wasn't yet two. I was raised by a couple who also couldn't have kids. They were good to me."

"You were never adopted?"

"No, the Pattersons only fostered. A lot of kids circled through their home. I was one of three long-termers."

"Where are they now? The Pattersons?"

Meghan looked up into the star-filled sky. "They are with their Creator."

5

Tom motioned for Ava to sit with him on the sofa. She wiped her hands on the kitchen towel and headed his way. As soon as she folded beside him, the tension she'd been carrying seemed to melt away. He had that effect on her. His ability to help her shed the cares of the world simply by his presence was one of the many things she loved about him.

Ava dropped her head against his chest and sighed. "What a night."

He kissed the top of her hair. "The evening certainly held some surprises." He squeezed her shoulder. "What's the matter, sweetheart? What's worrying you?"

"Did you notice Christel's face when Evan suggested they care for the babies?"

"It's understandable she might have some reservations. That's a lot to take on, especially when the situation came as such a surprise. Most of us need time to adjust to major life changes. Your daughter is no different."

Ava nodded. "Yeah, I suppose you're right. But I'm her mom. I saw something deeper."

"Like?"

"Like pure fear."

~

AFTER AN AWKWARD DRIVE home with Evan chattering excitedly and Christel sitting in silence, Evan pulled into their driveway and cut the engine. Without a word, Christel climbed from the car and took a deep breath. The night sky overhead twinkled with stars, a vast expanse reminding her that nothing was in her control. She turned and took hold of the handle on the backseat door, willing her hands to stop trembling.

There was no explaining how she felt, the terror building in her gut as she considered what was before her. In a weak moment, she'd let herself get swept up in the moment and agreed to bring them home. Her emotions had betrayed her.

Yes, she wanted a baby. Her baby.

Never had she considered mothering someone else's child. Correction, children. As in two babies. Twins.

Everyone expected her to be happy about having these babies land in her lap as if it were a miracle. Instead of feeling elation, her head kept reminding herself she was nothing but a temporary babysitter. Odds were, the mother would come to her senses and show up, wanting her children back. Christel had a law degree and knew how the courts worked. Parental rights trumped all else in nearly every situation, excluding abuse situations. Even then, she'd known of cases where children were returned to their biological parents.

She'd reluctantly agreed to care for these tiny babies—temporarily—but she would never fasten her heart. How could she possibly bear loving these twins only to face losing them?

First thing in the morning, she planned to take Evan aside and firmly explain her decision. There were trained foster parents who were much better equipped. They had resources available and were on board with parental reunification when appropriate. She'd make her husband understand he'd allowed his emotions to override his judgment.

Over the top of the car, Evan beamed in her direction. "Can you believe this, honey?" He opened the door and tackled the chore of unbuckling the little boy from the car seat the hospital had provided.

She pulled on her passenger side door and did likewise, taking care not to wake the sleeping baby girl. As Christel lifted the infant from the seat and into her arms, she couldn't miss the smell of baby powder. The scent caused her stomach to retract in a deep ache—a sad reminder of her failure to get pregnant.

She followed Evan inside and stood there, unsure of what to do next.

Evan seemed oblivious to her angst. He grinned and leaned over the tiny girl she carried. "Isn't she beautiful?" he asked, scrutinizing her features. "She's so tiny."

He returned his gaze to the little boy in his own arms. "What are we going to name them?"

Christel stiffened. "Name them?"

Her husband nodded. "We can't very well call them Baby A and Baby B."

"Why not? Their mother should be the one to name them."

"Their mother abandoned them, meaning she's out of the picture," he reminded. "In cases like these, where a parent drops their child off at a safe place, it's done with careful forethought."

"You mean desperation," she answered back as the baby in her arms startled. Her little face scrunched, and her mouth opened, letting out a loud cry.

Evan laughed. "Despite her tiny size, she sure has a set of lungs."

Christel pulled the baby to her shoulder and patted her

back. Despite her efforts to calm the infant, she continued to cry.

Evan leaned down for the bag the staff at the hospital had packed for them. "I think she's hungry." He laid the baby he was holding on a soft blanket and then headed for the kitchen with a bottle in his hand. He opened the door to the microwave, calling over his shoulder. "First thing in the morning, we'll go buy some things. Some bassinets, clothing, feeding supplies."

Christel couldn't help herself. She instinctively shook her head. "No. That's not a good idea."

Evan turned to face her. "What do you mean?"

"I mean, you need to slow down here. We have to discuss all this before we get into this situation too far." She drew a breath and tried to steady her building nerves. "Evan, you never asked me before jumping on this path. Yes, these babies needed care. Perhaps the better thing would have been to leave them at the hospital."

Evan frowned. "You know that's not how this works. The authorities would have placed them in foster care. We simply stepped up and filled that role. Luckily, as a licensed doctor, I am not subject to all the mountains of paperwork and background checks." His face broke into another smile. "This is our lucky break, Christel. Don't you see?"

She stood silent, holding the baby, who had now quit crying.

"Christel?"

"I can't, Evan." Her eyes filled with tears. "I just can't."

He rushed to her side and folded her into his arms, taking care not to press against the baby. "Talk to me, Christel."

Tears now streamed down her cheeks. "I'm afraid."

"Afraid of what, sweetheart?"

"She'll come back. She'll want them back."

He paused just long enough for Christel to know that as

much as he wanted to assure her that she was wrong, the possibility did exist.

"I couldn't bear it," she told him. "I would never survive loving these babies and then losing them."

6

Aiden grabbed his toolbox from the back of his truck as Shane pulled up next to him. His brother cut the motor and waved from his topless Jeep. "Hey, bro!"

Aiden nodded. "Thought you said you couldn't help?"

Shane slipped out of his Jeep. "Mom agreed to watch Carson. So, I'm all yours."

Their good friend, Ori, crossed the grass heading their way. "You guys are the best. I appreciate you lending a hand."

Aiden waved off the buddy he'd known since childhood. "Happy to help, Ori."

Shane followed the guys inside. "So, I think a case can be made for getting us out of the talent show. I mean, building the stage is our contribution, right?"

Aiden patted his misguided brother on the shoulder. "Yeah, let me know how that goes over with Mom."

Ka Hale A Ke Ola Resource Center was located north of Pā'ia on the Road to Hana. Ori served as director and lived behind the center in what Willa claimed was a treehouse. True, the structure was built high off the ground in the middle of thick tropical foliage, giving the appearance of a tree house. A long set of stairs led up to the single-room structure, which was painted green on the outside. The area underneath his place served as storage, where Ori parked his motorized scooter next to his surfboard. An unlocked cabinet held his fishing poles and gear, never seeming to worry about theft—or the fact he lived such a pared-down life.

"I don't need much," Ori often said. "Not when others don't even have a bed at night."

With the help of his father, who pastored Wailea Seaside Chapel, Ori started a nonprofit organization and opened the center right after he graduated from high school.

Ka Hale A Ke Ola had been breaking the cycle of homelessness on the island of Maui ever since. The center provided emergency shelter, life skills training, and provided a medical clinic, and facilities for child care—a true hand-up to people who honestly needed help.

Aiden placed his toolbox on the floor. "So, where do you want us to start?" It looked like someone had already erected the frame of what would become the stage at one end of the main hall.

"A good place to start is to get out your hammer."

Aiden turned to find Meghan standing there wearing a leather tool belt slung low on her hips. Her long dark hair was pulled back into a ponytail, and a red bandana was tied at her neck.

She parked her hands on her hips. "What are you staring at?"

Aiden cleared his throat and blinked. "Uh, nothing." Truth was, he could barely divert his attention.

Shane leaned close and whispered. "Look away, bro."

"Huh?" Aiden turned to his brother, who wore a stupid grin —the one he often displayed when he thought he had figured out a situation no one else had clued in on.

Aiden rolled his eyes and brushed off Shane's misplaced

assumption. Every hot girl was a prospect to his younger brother. It wasn't like that with Meghan. She was his co-worker. Friend.

Still, he couldn't ignore the way he felt when she smiled at him. "So, this is a surprise," he muttered, remembering the way she smelled last night.

"What? You don't think a girl is capable of building things?" she challenged.

"Just the opposite." He knew Meghan could do almost anything she set her mind to. "Nope. I just wasn't sure if you could pull yourself from stargazing long enough," he teased.

Meghan huffed and cocked her head. "Have you looked outside? Last time I gazed up into the sky, the only thing I saw was the sun. I mean, if you're seeing stars, Aiden, we'd best call your brother-in-law to come and medically check you out."

Shane watched them banter wearing a wisecrack smile.

Aiden knew what his brother was thinking. He'd have to set him straight later.

Ori clapped his hands together. "Well, regardless of stars or sun, there's a lot of work ahead. I'm grateful for the help."

Over the next hours, the four of them nailed planks of wood to the frame. Aiden found himself glancing over at Meghan more than once. She had a mouthful of nails between her lips, pulling them one-by-one and expertly wielding her hammer, driving each into the wood with only a couple of well-placed strokes.

He normally didn't care for defined muscles on a woman. Meghan wore them well, especially her toned upper arms. Soft skin covering steel.

A little like her.

Meghan McCord was as smart as his sister, Christel. Nothing got by her. She was as resourceful as Katie, making do in every situation, even when she had limited tools at her disposal. Once, she'd used one of her shoelaces covered with peanut butter to lure a frightened dog from a mangled car.

His mother's characteristic ability to negotiate any situation was also inherent in Meghan. Few situations set her off her game. Yet, there was something more, something he couldn't quite put his finger on.

Whatever it was, she was coming to mind far too often.

Thinking about her seemed a guilty pleasure. One he knew he should clamp down and guard against even a hint of impropriety. He'd dog-eared page 82 of the manual, where it clearly stated there should be no fraternization between the director and those he managed.

He went for beers with the guys all the time. Meghan often joined them. He could argue there was no difference. She was one of the team...that's all.

Whom was he kidding?

What he'd recently been thinking about Meghan was a far cry from anything that circled his head regarding any of the guys at the station.

She bent over to grab another 4x4.

The fact was, none of them looked that good in a pair of jeans.

Aiden shook his head and exhaled loudly. Nor did they fill out the front of their shirts as well.

Yeah, there was that.

7

C hristel woke with a start. Disoriented, she glanced around to see where the knocking was coming from.

The door. The sound was coming from the door.

A glance at her Apple watch revealed it was after seven. She'd slept in and was late for work.

Christel groaned and ran her hand over the top of her hair before she remembered.

She'd been up several times throughout the night. Babies had to be fed every few hours, and the orphaned infants seemed to be on opposite schedules regarding their hunger. Evan got up with her for the first shift, but he had an elbow reconstruction surgery this morning that couldn't be rescheduled. He had to get sleep. So, the remainder of the night shift fell to her.

"Coming," she yelled before she realized her loud voice might wake the babies. Too late. Shrieks came from one of the temporary bassinets they'd made out of emptied dresser drawers. She hurried for the door.

She flung it open to find her mother standing there with a wide smile. "Good morning, sweetheart."

Christel didn't bother to hold back a second groan. "No, it isn't."

Her mom leaned in and kissed her cheek. "Up all night?"

Christel refrained from delivering a snarky answer. Instead, she headed for the kitchen while her mother quickly moved for the dresser drawer beds. She bent and lifted the tiny boy with a set of powerful lungs and brought him to her shoulder. Like an expert, she patted his little bottom and crooned. "There, there...that's it."

He quieted instantly.

"Oh, honey. You look like you didn't get a wink last night." Her voice sounded sympathetic, even while her eyes twinkled in that certain way—as if she secretly appreciated how her own daughter now understood what she had suffered as a young mom—a sisterhood of sorts.

Christel scooped extra coffee grounds into her espresso machine. Time to bring on the double shot.

"Oh, these babies are so precious," her mother cooed. "What are you naming them?"

"We're not." Christel pulled her favorite mug from the cupboard. "You want some coffee?"

Her mother shook her head. "No thanks, dear. Why aren't you naming them? Someone has to. You can't call them—"

"Baby A and Baby B. Yes, I've been told."

Her mother's eyebrows drew together in a concerned frown. "Christel, what's the matter? Talk to me."

Perhaps it was exhaustion or pure frustration—she didn't know. All she knew was that she couldn't muster the emotional fortitude to hide her emotions. "These babies are not a substitution for the one I've been trying to conceive," she explained, a little more terse than she wanted.

"No one seems to get the reality of the situation." Her eyes filled with jaded tears. "I am simply a babysitter, an unwilling one at that," she quietly admitted. "Evan—well, he thinks otherwise."

"Oh. I see."

She looked at her mom with desperation. "I can't do it, Mom."

"Do what, honey?"

"I am not their mother. They have a mother."

Ava dropped her gaze to the infant in her arms. After several long moments, she finally voiced a reply. "No one is ever ready for this role, Christel. Becoming a parent means saying goodbye to your heart, knowing the risk. There's a lot out there to be afraid of."

She laid the baby back down and turned to her daughter, motioning for her to join her on the sofa.

Christel reluctantly obeyed.

Ava drew her against her. "As a mom, you lie awake at night, surrounded by monsters of possibilities that you've never considered: choking on a jelly bean accidentally left on the floor, electrocution when they stick something in an uncovered electrical outlet, or getting burned by pulling a boiling pot off the stove. The worry doesn't end when they grow up. Now you fret about drunk drivers on the street, child molesters in the bathroom, other dysfunctional kids in the neighborhood—the list never ends."

She squeezed Christel's shoulder. "As a mother, are you supposed to just shut all that off? It's impossible. You simply try to push the fears aside and pray for the best."

Her mother knew her so well...every proud moment and every fear. She'd seen right through her protests to the terror she harbored inside.

"What if she changes her mind, Mom?" She swallowed the block of concrete forming in her throat. "I couldn't bear losing them."

Her mother slowly nodded. "True, but the possibility of

losing your babies always exists, honey. None of us are promised tomorrow. Our family learned that hard truth not so long ago when your dad passed away. The fact is, I could lose any one of you kids at any time. I have to trust that God is in control."

"But if God had wanted me to be a mother, He would've made me pregnant," Christel argued.

A slow smile sprouted on her mom's face. "Or maybe He planned a blessing you never saw coming."

8

W illa closed her textbook and climbed from her bed. With her homework finished, she wandered downstairs to find a note on the counter from her mom.

"Honey, I didn't want to interrupt your schoolwork, but I had to run over to the gift shop for a while and then to the office to meet Uncle Evan. I'll be back in a few hours. I have Noelle with me. Would you make us some dinner? Dad is working late tonight, so make something simple. Grilled cheese and tomato soup, maybe? Thanks, baby."

Usually, Willa would get annoyed at the request. A full day of class and then hours of writing a paper on the causes, effects, and consequences of earthquakes left her little time for fun. When was she going to finish watching *Gilmore Girls* on Netflix?

All her friends were watching *Stranger Things*, but her mom and dad were lame and wouldn't allow her to watch the popular series. Neither would Kina's mom. She said it had too much foul language for impressionable young minds.

She would be glad when she was eighteen and could shed all these restrictions and live how she wanted.

Willa crumpled the note and tossed it in the trash before heading for the refrigerator. Inside was a thawed chicken. She pulled the platter from the shelf and set it on the counter, then she lifted her phone and went to Pinterest, her mom's favorite place to find recipes. She typed "chicken" and scrolled through the listings until she landed on a photo of what they called Marry Me Chicken.

That looked delicious!

She scanned the ingredient list and checked the refrigerator and cupboards. She had everything she needed—cream, garlic, parmesan cheese, sundried tomatoes, and olive oil. Why make boring grilled cheese sandwiches when she could assemble something far more appetizing? Her dad would be so impressed!

She'd never cut up a chicken, but how hard could it be?

Not hard, she discovered. Thankfully, her chef dad had great knives.

Willa had just slid the pan of ingredients into the oven and turned on the timer when her phone rang. She picked up.

"Hey, girl."

"Kina! What's up?"

Willa explained that she had just made dinner for her family. "There's enough that I think I'll have Mom give some to Uncle Evan to take home so that Aunt Christel doesn't have to cook. I'm sure her hands have been full handling those new babies."

"That's nice of you," Kina said. "Can you believe someone dropped off two babies at Maui Emergency Services?"

"Yeah, Grammy Ava says there's something called the Safe Haven Law which allows any parent to surrender their child with no questions asked. The rule is supposed to keep desperate people from putting babies in trash dumpsters or something worse."

"And they don't get in trouble?"

"No, even if they wish to disclose their identities, they are free from legal consequences. At least that's what Grammy Ava explained."

There was a brief pause on the other end of the phone. "But what if the other parent doesn't know? What if they don't consent to give up their babies?"

Willa pulled some lettuce and salad makings from the bottom drawer of their refrigerator. "Uncle Aiden says the authorities always check the Exploited and Missing Children database. If a baby is reported missing, the police know and reunite the child with its parent. This works for fathers, too. Uncle Aiden says it's a fail-safe thing."

"That's good."

"What is good is that Aunt Christel and Uncle Evan might be able to keep the babies. Just between us, I overheard my mom telling my dad that Aunt Christel couldn't get pregnant. I could have two new baby cousins in the family."

Willa placed the lettuce on the cutting board, grabbed the sharp knife from the counter, and chopped.

"I love when things work out like that," Kina said, clearly eating something.

"Is your mouth full?" Willa asked, starting on the radishes.

Her friend giggled. "Yeah, sorry."

"Look, I'd better go. I need to finish up dinner before my mom gets home."

"Wait! What are you wearing tomorrow?"

Willa smiled. They often coordinated outfits. "My pink shorts and that cute top I bought when Mom took us to the Shops at Wailea. The one with the little pink hearts."

"Ooh...that's so fire! I love that top." She quickly recited that she would wear something similar. "And my new Nizza Bonega's."

"The hi-tops with the yellow daisies you've been checking

out?" Willa asked, grabbing a carrot and placing it on the cutting board.

"Yup. I finally earned enough. If I have to mop one more floor at the Banana Patch, I'll bury my head under a pillow and never lift it again."

"I hear you."

"Okay, well, Mom's calling me. Guess I'll talk to you later tonight." Her friend bid her goodbye and clicked off.

Willa quickly texted her mom and told her what she was up to. "I made enough for Uncle Evan and Aunt Christel, too."

~

EVAN CAME through the door carrying an insulated bag. "Your sister sent dinner home with me," he told Christel. "Well, actually, your niece cooked for us. She said it was some kind of baked chicken dish and salad."

Christel looked at him and said nothing.

"Oh, honey. I'm sorry I didn't get home earlier."

"Yeah, I need a shower. They just ate. Now they are sleeping." She pointed to the kitchen sink piled high with dirty bottles and the counter cluttered with lidless containers of formula and half-drunk cups of cold coffee. "After my shower, I'm going to bed. You're up for the night shift." It wasn't a question, but a statement. If he wanted to be magnanimous and care for these abandoned babies, he'd be wise not to argue with her.

"Sure. Did you eat?"

She turned and ran her hand through the top of her unbrushed hair. "Huh? Oh, no. I ate some crackers."

"You have to eat more than that," Evan scolded.

"Sure, I'll eat something later. Right now, I need that shower and some sleep."

Hours later, she woke with a start. Someone was shaking her.

Christel groaned. "No, leave me be. I'm tired," she muttered. The last thing she wanted was to open her eyes right now.

"Honey? I need you to wake up."

The shaking motion, coupled with her husband's voice and the crying coming from the living room, pulled her from her slumber. "What?" she asked sleepily as she sat up.

"You need to get the babies," Evan said. "I'm sick."

"Sick? What kind of sick?"

He didn't answer her question. He simply ran for their bathroom and called over his shoulder, "My stomach."

Christel folded back the bed covers and pulled herself from the warm mattress. The bedside clock revealed it was three o'clock in the morning.

She hurried for the living room and glanced between the pseudo beds, aka drawers. Which one of them was crying?

The little boy.

She bent and picked him up, felt, and discovered he needed a diaper change.

"Shh...it's okay. I know. Wet diapers are nasty," she said to the little guy as she headed for the diaper bag. Finding it empty, she headed for the kitchen. The box was on the counter. So was the earlier mess.

Christel groaned. This parenting thing wasn't as easy as you'd think.

She headed for the sofa, where she diapered the baby. Intending to feed him, she moved back into the kitchen. Before she could finish making a bottle, the infant fell asleep. She smiled, returned to his bed, and laid him carefully on the receiving blanket. If she was lucky, she might be able to catch a few more minutes of sleep.

Christel leaned against the sofa cushions and shut her eyes only to open them seconds later when Evan entered the room.

"You okay?" she whispered so as not to awaken the babies.

Her husband shook his head. "I just came in to tell you I think I'd better leave, so I don't make the babies sick. Or you."

Before she could respond, Christel's phone buzzed. She picked it up to find a text from her sister.

"Did you eat the food we sent over?"

Christel scowled and tapped out a quick answer. "Why?"

The phone immediately rang, and Christel hurried to answer before the sound could wake the babies. "Why?" she repeated, without waiting to hear her sister's voice.

"I'm SO sorry. We're all sick over here. North and south, if you know what I mean."

"Sick? From what?"

"It appears Willa failed to listen to Jon's earlier lesson on the dangers of cross-contamination. Between trips to the bathroom, she admitted to using the same knife to chop lettuce as she'd used to cut up the chicken. Looks like a food-borne thing. Jon says it should pass in twenty-four hours."

"Well, that's great." Christel knew she didn't come off sounding the least bit gracious. She didn't care.

Then she remembered she hadn't eaten any of the food. "Oh, my goodness. I didn't eat any, but Evan did. He's heading for the toilet again now." She watched as her stricken husband hurried from the room, holding the back of his robe with one hand.

"Do you want me to call Mom and have her come over to help you with the babies?"

Christel shook her head. "No. I got it handled." True. Evan was out of commission and couldn't help her. That didn't mean she wasn't capable of dealing with the situation, especially since she did get some sleep earlier.

She got off the phone with her sister, wandered into the bathroom, and stood in the doorway. "Well, the good news is you don't have to leave. You're not contagious." She explained the situation.

"Well, that answers a lot," Evan said as he followed her out of the bathroom. His face was the color of cream of mushroom soup.

"You should get some sleep while you can," she told him.

Evan nodded. "Yeah, probably. Sorry," he said, apologizing yet again.

"Don't worry about it," she said. "I'll be in the living room if you need anything."

She made another try for the sofa and some much-needed rest, punching the decorative pillow and nestling her head against it. She had just closed her eyes when she heard a whimper.

Christel waited. Perhaps the baby, whichever one, would slip back to sleep if left undisturbed.

She closed her eyes again.

Another whimper.

Giving up, Christel straightened and headed for the drawer nearest the sofa. Inside, the itty-bitty girl had open eyes and was sucking furiously at her hand.

Christel couldn't help it. Her heart melted at the sight.

These babies were darling, especially this one.

She bent and lifted the little girl into her arms. "You hungry, sweetheart?" The term of endearment easily slipped from her lips, the same one her mother often used when addressing her —even as an adult.

Christel hurried and fixed a bottle, then slipped the soft rubber nipple inside the baby's lips. The baby hungrily drank down the warm liquid. Her nubbed infant toes peeked from the blanket prompting Christel to tuck the fabric more securely.

For months, Christel and Evan strived to conceive, wanting desperately to be granted the treasure of parenthood. Each month, disappointment loomed and robbed them of their dreams.

Who in their right mind could throw away such a gift?

Surely, the desperate woman would come to her senses and realize what she'd given up and change her mind. Christel simply couldn't imagine otherwise.

Christel lifted the bottle from the baby's mouth and set it on the sofa table, then placed the little girl on her shoulder and patted her back gently until a burp came.

"Ah, that's it." Surprisingly no longer exhausted, Christel lowered the baby to her lap and extended her pinky. The infant girl wrapped her tiny fingers around Christel's and hung on with surprising grip strength for someone so small.

Christel found herself barely able to breathe against the building ache. Look at how tiny, how vulnerable, how awe-inspiring.

Before she knew it, a tear escaped and ran down her cheek.

Their gazes met—that tiny little girl's and her own.

For so long, Christel fought waves of simmering anger that secretly dwelled inside. With each negative pregnancy test, she'd faced defeat—a door slamming closed on her dreams of being a mother.

She'd blamed herself for waiting so long. Blamed God for pushing the hold button on her plans, even worried His finger might be poised and ready to press the big NO forever.

She hated Evan for pushing. Yes, that was hard to admit— but it was true.

She resented her sister for having two darling daughters when she couldn't even have one. Ha—even Shane had been blessed with being a parent, while Evan tried to hide his disappointment every time Christel had to burst his hope bubble.

Jay's addiction became enemy number one. Things would have been different if it had not been for her former husband's illness.

None of her feelings were compatible with sound judgment. Emotions were like that...erratic and unexplained.

Nothing made any sense—only her wounded pride...and her bruised heart.

Christel gazed down at the baby. What would happen if her mother didn't return for her? These little ones would end up in foster care. Then what?

As if reading her mind, the infant girl tightened her grip, hanging onto Christel as if holding onto a lifeline—perhaps instinctively knowing what Christel failed to see.

An unusual awakening rose in her, so odd that it took her a minute to recognize it.

Her concrete composure crumbled. Tears streamed without inhibition.

Her mom was right. How had she failed to foresee how her unspoken prayers might be answered?

Her heart pounded with the knowledge deep inside that everything would work out. There were no accidents in life. Everything happens for a reason.

She swallowed her fear.

"Don't worry, little one," she murmured in a choked voice. She drew the baby to her chest and savored the feel of the faint heartbeat. "No matter what the future holds, I'll take care of you and your brother," she whispered against the tiny ear. "You are safe and wanted."

She and Evan would cross the legal hurdles. They were meant to be parents. Negative pregnancy tests had failed to erase the deepest desire in their hearts. They both longed to have children and a family. What they had not known is that a plan to grant their wishes had always been in place.

She rocked the little girl gently back and forth. "Mommy will always be here."

Christel kissed the top of her new daughter's head.

"Forever."

9

Evan looked down at his sleeping wife on the sofa. Both babies were nestled in her arms, also sleeping. Concern pulled at his brows.

The babies could easily slide to the floor, and his exhausted wife would be too tired to wake and catch them. The sweet smile on her face swayed him from scolding her.

He bent and gently lifted the baby boy.

Christel's eyes flew open at the first movement.

"I'm sorry, honey. I didn't mean to wake you." He brushed a strand of hair from her forehead and planted a kiss. "I'll take over if you want to go back to bed and get some sleep."

Christel's face brightened with a wide smile. She slowly sat up, taking care not to wake the remaining baby in her arms.

She patted the space next to her. "Sit; we've got to talk."

He complied with her wishes.

"We need to name our babies," she said, grinning.

It took a moment for her words to sink in. "Our babies?"

She slowly nodded, beaming.

"What are you saying?"

She told him about the epiphany that came in the middle of

the night. "Mom was so right. I always assumed I'd become a parent by first getting pregnant. I was foolish to box God in like that."

He couldn't help it. His hand went to his mouth as he let the notion sink in. Christel had changed her mind and was willing to pursue the adoption of the babies. He could barely breathe for the joy that welled inside.

There was a time he could barely lift his head from the pillow. After Tess was killed in Iraq, he'd frankly wanted to die, too. The fact that she was carrying his son at the time of the helicopter crash only deepened the loss.

The emotional wounds were deep.

In time, he'd been able to stuff the hurt and move on.

His life here was a one-hundred-eighty-degree turn from serving in the military, especially when he was deployed. Doctors working in an environment of armed conflict face situations where patients have overwhelming injuries. There was often limited access to medical resources to provide treatment. And the doctors themselves could often be in danger. The stress of all of that could suck a person dry.

Even when he'd served stateside, he couldn't seem to fill that deep hole in his spirit—the chasm that formed from all the times he'd had to declare a situation futile, knowing that a mother, a father, perhaps a wife, was going to feel what he'd felt in losing Tess. That deep pain and loss of knowing the end had come. There would never be another see you later. No more phone calls. No more shared meals. For those who were married, no more shared beds.

Evan was very good at two things...the practice of medicine and hiding his inner pain. No one knew the toll those months had taken.

Then he met Christel.

The day he walked into the hospital waiting room to deliver

the results of her brother's surgery after the boat explosion replaced his despair with a glimmer of hope.

The way she looked at him nearly stopped his heart from beating. No woman had instantly prompted that forgotten longing, the tingles that travel up your spine at the very sight of her.

Something else pulled his heartstrings. The weariness in her gaze as she pummeled him with questions about her brother's status. He saw past her competent can-do attitude and became startled by the sadness in her eyes. He recognized that sort of buried hurt. The deep beckoned the deep...and his heart yearned to answer the call.

Never had he thought he could be truly happy again. Yet, before he knew it, they stood on the rocky bluff overlooking the ocean, saying "I do" and committing their lives to one another.

Never had he been filled with such elation. The highs are higher when you've experienced the lows.

Of course, another emotional plummet followed when he walked into their bathroom months later and found her sobbing with another negative pregnancy test in her shaking hands. He'd so desperately wanted to fix the situation, make things better. Hell, he'd tried to give her the world.

Unfortunately, he was helpless. He couldn't give her a baby. He couldn't make her a mother. Even when he offered medical solutions, she turned down procedures that might alter the situation.

He'd been forced to face the truth. As badly as he wanted to fix this...he was impotent to do so.

When these abandoned babies showed up, Evan was confident these infants were the answer. He and Christel needed children. These children needed a family.

How much clearer could it be?

Still, he sensed he shouldn't push too far too fast, and for a good reason.

It was clear that Christel was terrified of opening the flood-gates, revealing the depth of her fear. She seemed really, truly afraid for the first time in her life. Nothing he could say would be able to assuage that fear. He knew that.

He needed to step back and let this situation run its course, admit to himself it might be possible these babies were not the answer to their dilemma.

Now, this.

Evan drew a deep breath. Had he even heard his wife correctly?

She laughed, knowing what was circling his brain. "Yes, Evan...*our* babies. Honey, I want to adopt them." She tilted her head to look up at him. "Say something."

He grinned back at her, so happy he could barely contain the joy. "If that's the case, we should come up with some names."

Christel's expression broke into a wide grin. "How about Janie and Jenner?"

"Janie and Jenner Matisse. I love it!"

Evan's phone rang. He quickly pulled it from his robe pocket and brought it to his ear. "Aiden, buddy. What's up?"

A heavy moment of silence followed.

Aiden cleared his throat. "Uh, the mom showed back up at the station. I think you'd better bring the babies back. We've called the authorities. They're on their way."

10

Christel sat stonelike in the front seat of Evan's car, willing herself not to fall apart.

How could she have been so stupid?

Only a fool would let her guard down and jump headlong into this abyss when the babies' mother could change her mind and want these children back. The statistics were high that mothers offering up their children for adoption often experienced severe remorse in the early hours and reversed their decision. Christel had pushed all that aside and let her emotions carry her away.

Now, she would pay the price.

Evan reached for her hand.

She quietly pulled it back. She didn't want his comfort. She didn't want anyone's comfort. All she wanted was to get through this.

"Honey?"

Christel held up an open palm. "Evan, don't."

She was being insensitive and selfish. Her husband was disappointed and hurting, too. Yet, it was his anger that surprised her most. "Why would child services give these babies back to someone who didn't want them?"

Didn't want them.

Christel's gut wrenched. Only hours ago, she'd held Janie in her arms, vowed to keep her safe, and told her she would always be wanted. She had no way of keeping either of those promises. Her emotions—the deep desire for a child—well, she'd allowed her judgment to fade.

Janie and Jenner, or whatever their names would now be, would never remember her promises...never remember her.

She would never forget.

~

AVA GRABBED her bag and dialed Katie on her way out of the office.

"What's up, Mom?"

Ava explained the situation. "Christel and Evan are on their way to meet child services at their office. Meet me there. I know Christel. Any veneer she erects will only be a cover-up. Giving these babies back will crush her."

"I thought Christel was pushing back on stepping in to care for these abandoned twins?" Katie argued. "She had no interest in anything formal regarding keeping these children, right?"

"If you think that, you don't know your sister very well."

"I'll call Shane."

"No need," Ava told her youngest daughter. "I already reached out to him. He and Jack are on their way. Mig's covering things for me here. I'm not sure how long sorting all this out will take, but she'll need her family." She recited the address. "See you there."

Ava hung up with a sinking feeling building in her gut. There wasn't much to sort out. In less than forty-eight hours, the mother had shown back up. Unless there were good reasons not to restore her parental rights, the babies would be returned.

She supposed reunification, when called for, was a good thing. She truly wanted what was best for those sweet babies.

She also wanted what was best for her baby...her grown baby who wanted a baby of her own and had been unable to conceive. The cruelty of having her daughter's hope ripped away was not lost on Ava. Nor was the part she had played in that.

Foolishly, she'd urged Christel to consider how God might provide in ways unimagined. She still believed in answered prayer. Apparently, these abandoned babies were not His plan.

Another disappointment of this magnitude would surely contaminate her daughter's belief that she was destined to be a mother. Christel would act stoic and sturdy, but this would wobble and make her unsteady inside.

Which is why her family would drop everything and be there to support her. The Briscoes were altruistic in their steadfast love for one another. They'd taken many hits. Together, they'd weathered many things and came out standing.

Surrounded by her family, Christel would make it through this setback.

∾

EVAN AND CHRISTEL couldn't find a parking spot for all the familiar cars parked on the street in front of child services. Her mother's car, her sister's vehicle, and Shane's Jeep took up the available space.

An immediate frown formed on Christel's face. "Looks like we'll be doing this with an audience."

Evan pointed out a sign that said an additional lot was located at the back of the building. "It's all right. We'll park there."

She nodded numbly. "Okay."

When he killed the engine, she looked over at him. "Let's get this over with as quickly as possible. I mean it, Evan. No drama."

"Honey, you don't necessarily have to go in and be part of this. Do you want to stay in the car?"

For a brief moment, she considered accepting his offer. It would be cruel to expect him to face what was ahead without her by his side. "No. I'm good. Besides, what are you going to do? Carry two babies?" Then, to brighten the mood, she added, "Let's go to dinner after. Maybe Mom and the others would like to join us. I'm okay with that, so long as this meeting is not a topic of discussion." The faster she could emotionally move on from this disappointment, the better.

"Whatever you want, babe."

They both climbed from the car and turned to the back seat to retrieve the babies. Despite her stoic resolve, Christel could barely breathe as she unbuckled Janie and lifted her into her arms. She was warm and smelled of baby powder.

Christel bit the inside of her cheek to keep her emotions in check.

"C'mon, little buddy." Evan lifted the tiny boy into his embrace and brushed his lips across the top of his fuzzy head. "You're going to be fine. You will be loved."

"Do we know that?" Christel looked away as her husband circled the car. "I mean, none of this makes sense. A mother abandons her babies only to show up and ask for them back. What does that say?"

Evan gently touched her arm. "It says she wants them." He blinked away his own emotion. "That's a good thing, Christel." He took her free hand in his own. "I've given this a lot of thought since getting that call. We want what is best for these little ones. If the mom wants them, we have to believe that is the best thing."

She nodded. "You're right." She took a deep breath. What Evan claimed was indeed true. They needed to believe the best in this situation. For their mental well-being, they would relinquish their concerns and embrace the possibility that the mom deeply loved and wanted her babies. Panic can cause people to make rash judgments.

Situations like these were never simply black and white. The Safe Haven law allows a short time for a parent to change their mind for this very reason.

She should focus on being grateful that this was happening sooner than later. Had she and Evan bonded further with these little ones, their hearts would undoubtedly suffer far more damage.

Evan dropped her hand and reached for the doorknob. He turned it and pushed the door open, stepping back so she could enter.

Inside, the small lobby was crowded with her family. Ava immediately stood and drew her into a shoulder hug. "Honey, we're all here for you."

Christel turned her gaze upon her family members, surprised to see Uncle Jack among them. "Thanks, I appreciate it."

The statement wasn't a lie. She did treasure their support. She only wished she could face this hard thing free of the watchful eyes of family, no matter how well-intentioned. She didn't want her emotions measured and weighed.

Shane gave her a wink. "I know that look. We won't intrude. Promise."

Katie and Ava both nodded.

"Yes, we're only here for you," her mother assured. "Whatever you need, baby."

Aiden silently took his mom and sister by the elbows and guided them to a sofa with worn cushions. They sat, and so did he. Shane found a spot and dropped to the floor. He sat cross-legged and leaned against the wall.

Uncle Jack pursed his lips and studied the bubbling aquarium filled with neon tetras and beta fish with long blue tails draped behind them.

Was that a tear she saw forming in his eyes?

"Stop it, all of you. Yes, this isn't what we expected, but these babies have a mother, and she wants them. That's a good thing." Christel swallowed, hoping her announcement would shift the focus from her disappointment.

Evan was quick to agree. "We need to support this reunification."

A door opened, and a woman appeared carrying a folder in her hand and wearing a smile. She seemed to be in her late fifties and was dressed in brown pants with a pretty white top with tiny ruffles along the button placket.

Her blonde hair had turned nearly silver and was cut in a trendy, short spiky style with one side tucked behind her ear. Earrings dangled from her lobes, and her lips were a pretty fuchsia.

"Thank you for coming in," she said as she moved to Evan and Christel. "And for watching over these little ones. We do not take the donation of your time and care lightly." She scanned the room and nodded with approval. "Clearly, selfless contribution runs in your family."

She tucked the folder under one arm and peered at the little boy in Evan's arms. "I'm Maggie Williams, the caseworker."

Brief introductions were made before she motioned to the open door behind her. "Let's have you join me in my office."

Christel and Evan followed her down a short hallway. Christel was filled with questions but couldn't voice a single one as they entered a room to the left. It was as if she were on autopilot.

Evan cleared his throat. "What happens now?"

Christel found her voice. "The mother—is she here?"

Maggie lifted the manila folder. "I have news to share."

"What news?" Evan asked, frowning.

"The mother wants to formally relinquish."

Christel stopped breathing. "What?"

Evan's frown deepened with confusion. "What are you saying? We thought she—"

"Wanted the babies back?" Maggie shook her head. "No. That's not the case."

Maggie's bright-colored lips widened into a smile. "I have the signed papers here. The next step is for me to present them to the judge. Temporary guardianship will be granted. At the end of the fourteen days, providing you still want full custody, we will ask for an expedited hearing, and you will become new parents." Before they could respond, she placed the manila folder on her tidy desk and opened it. "You are both licensed professionals, meaning the background check process should go quickly."

"Of course, we want them!" Christel blurted.

She handed Evan a pen. "Excellent. I thought that to be the case. We only need you to sign some paperwork, and we'll do our job and get these tiny babies adopted." She grinned at them.

Speechless, Evan and Christel stared at each other in disbelief.

"This is my favorite part of the job," Maggie admitted.

"This is excellent news!" Evan finally exclaimed.

"But, what about the mother?" Still wary, Christel had a driving need for information. "Who is she? Where is she?"

"I'm afraid I can't release those details," Maggie told them. "The mother wants her identity to remain undisclosed. This will be a closed adoption." She gave Christel a sympathetic look. "I can tell you that she is not a permanent resident and will be leaving the island very soon."

"And the father?"

"He's recently deceased." She held up what looked to be a copy of a death certificate from the file. "A car accident. He was married—to someone else. The birth mother is young and now wishes to return to school and get on with her life without disclosing the situation to people she believes would be hurt by it. That's really all I can say."

Things were becoming clear, prompting Christel's heart to fill with compassion. Her hand shook as she signed the paperwork. "So, that's it? That's all you need from us?"

"For now," Maggie told her. "Thankfully, the birth mother made good choices. Many desperate young women don't. That's why we have the Safe Haven law in place. In this case, we are fortunate she reconsidered and came forward willing to sign the paperwork that will hasten your ability to adopt."

Maggie hesitated. "And one more thing." She pulled a sealed envelope from the file and handed it to Christel. "She wanted you both to have this."

With shaking hands, Christel took the envelope and opened it. Inside was a handwritten letter, the writing neat and on plain white paper. A few of the letters were marred with what appeared to be tear stains.

By now, you know my story. Please don't hate me. I'm a good person. I simply got caught in a situation I never thought I'd face. I've embraced a solution I think is the best for everyone involved.

I want you to know I love these babies. I've been watching you both over the past couple of days. You seem to be good people...a couple who desperately wants children.

For that reason, I am convinced I made the best choice.

Take care of them. Tell them I loved them enough to do what was best for them, even if my own heart broke.

One more thing...please love them well for me and be the family I

could not provide. There will not be a night I lay my head on the
pillow to go to sleep that I won't think of you all.

The letter was signed off with two tiny hand-drawn hearts.

The impact of what had just happened hit Christel. She looked over at Evan and openly wept.

An unknown woman had sacrificed her heart. Because of that, her own dreams were coming true.

She was finally going to be a mother.

11

A little over two weeks later, the adoption was finalized. Evan and Christel were granted permanent custody of Janie and Jenner. As was typical, the Briscoe family gathered at the courthouse to be part of the big event.

Aiden hung back and watched as his mother pulled his sister into a tight tug. "I told you God would come through, sweetheart."

Outside, they were met with a sidewalk filled with more well-wishers, including Alani, Ori, and Elta. Alani held a massive bouquet of pink and blue balloons in her hand. "You are all coming to Te Au Kane Luau this afternoon for a celebratory luau."

Elta grinned. "My wife has been preparing since the wee hours of the morning."

"No slowing down this one," Ori added, pulling his mother into a shoulder hug. "You would never guess this woman battled cancer only a few months ago."

Aiden took it all in, closing his eyes. He loved when a story ended well.

His sister had been through a lot. He'd watched her release

her grip on her first marriage after several years of struggling to fix someone who wasn't hers to fix. In the aftermath of the divorce, Christel buried herself in her work at Pali Maui. Balance sheets and profit and loss statements became her solace, her grip on a new life she never asked for.

Aiden had played a small role in turning the tide on her loneliness. He never chose to be in that boating accident. The aftermath and rehabilitation were grueling. Yet, Dr. Matisse had ended up his brother-in-law...something he never saw coming.

The entire family marveled to see her so happy again. Then she and Evan decided to try for a family.

The contentment on his sister's face had slowly transformed back into sadness as months passed, and she was unable to get pregnant. Who would have thought babies left at the station would change all that?

Aiden shook his head in amazement.

His mom was right. Things had a way of working out in unexpected and marvelous ways.

～

THE LUAU WAS everything Alani promised it would be. Not only was Christel surprised to see so many family members and friends gathered to help her and Evan celebrate their new family, but the food was amazing.

She shouldn't have been surprised. Alani's luau was known as the best on the island. The reservation list was months long.

Katie approached, holding Noelle against her hip. The little girl pointed at the baby boy in Christel's arms. "I hold the baby," she said, reaching for Jenner. "I hold him."

Katie brushed a kiss on the top of her toddler's head. "I'm afraid you're too little. You can kiss him, though."

Noelle scowled. "I not too little." Despite her protests, she gave up the idea proposed and leaned forward to give her new cousin a kiss.

"Gentle," Katie warned.

With utmost care, Noelle carefully placed her lips against the baby's head. She lifted her face and followed the kiss with a light pat of her dimpled hand. "Aw...he so cute."

Shane appeared with Carson. Based on the way he kicked his chubby legs in excitement, he wanted in on the action. "Meet your new cousin," Shane told him. "I predict you two are going to take over Black Rock someday and show them who's boss. No pansy diving for these boys."

"Maybe they'll even get our signature tattoo." Their Aunt Vanessa held up the inside of her arm, which sported an inked image of a honu turtle, the same one Shane had on his shoulder. They'd gotten the tattoos at the same time not long after Vanessa moved to the island. The symbol had become even more significant and was perhaps a foreshadowing of the turtle rescue she now directed with her daughter Isabelle's help.

"Hey, Aunt Vanessa. Thanks for coming," Christel said, beaming.

"Give me that baby," Vanessa said with extended arms. "I haven't even had the chance to hold him yet."

Isabelle peered over her shoulder. "Oh, isn't he cute?"

"Yes, he sure is. But don't you go getting any ideas. It's going to be a long while before you have one of these...right?"

Her daughter laughed. "A long, long time."

They all lined up to fill their plates. An entire kalua pig had been pulled from an underground oven in an elaborate imu ceremony. The cooking pit used a combination of hot coals, stones, and layers of coconut palm leaves to steam the pork, which was then transported to the serving table by bare-chested native men wearing lavalava cloths around their waists.

Evan came up alongside Christel. "Where's Jenner?"

"Aunt Vanessa absconded with him," she said, pulling little

Janie from his arms. "I'll hold her so you can fill a plate." She smiled to herself. How long would it be before they could actually eat together again?

"You don't have to offer twice," Evan pointed at the long tables. "Alani outdid herself."

Christel wholeheartedly agreed. In addition to the kalua pork, there was lomilomi salmon, poi taro rolls, sauteed gingered mahi, and one of Christel's personal favorites...baked honey coconut glazed purple sweet potato. Her mouth watered, thinking about the luxurious sweetness.

As Evan headed off to fill his plate, Christel motioned to get his attention. "Hey, honey. When was the last time she was changed?"

Her sleep-deprived husband looked to the sky in thought. "Uh, it's been a while. You might check her."

Christel nodded and headed for a spot beneath a tall palm gently waving in the sea breeze. She opened her bag, retrieved a waterproof mat, and laid it on the ground. It had only been a short while since the twins had landed in their home. Already she'd mastered the art of holding a baby in her arm while doing whatever was necessary with her free one.

"Hey, there."

She looked up to see Shane. "Where's Carson?"

"Mom."

She nodded and patted the ground beside her. "In that case, sit."

He did as she beckoned and handed her a baby wipe from the package. "It's something, isn't it?"

"What do you mean?"

"I mean, no one tells you exactly what it's like. You can imagine being a parent, or in my case, refuse to imagine...and then it happens. In a moment, everything changes. Your entire world slips into this place where your heart is no longer your own. You eat, breathe, and think of little else but your kid." Her little brother shook his head. "If someone had told me all that was on the horizon, I might have been filled with dread. I'd have been so off base. No one can fully describe the way your heart fills and nearly bursts with such immense...I dunno, joy. That kid is yours...to mold, to train, to protect. Yours." He shook his head a second time. "Amazing."

Christel unfastened Janie's wet diaper. "Who are you, and what did you do with my little brother?"

"Seriously, sis. Who would have expected things would turn out like this for us? I mean, I was really hurting after Dad died. I guess I tried to fill the hole inside with a few bed romps... know what I mean? I didn't expect to fall for Aimee. When she left me all alone with Carson, I was in the worst pain I'd ever felt."

"You hid it well."

He shrugged. "It's what guys do."

Their mom approached, holding Carson's hand and patiently walking beside the toddler. "Hey, you two, aren't you going to eat?"

They both smiled in her direction. "Sure."

Carson giggled and ran into Shane's arms. "Da-da."

Christel finished up diapering her little daughter and handed the baby off to her mom. She turned to follow her and Shane back to the luau festivities when she spotted someone in the distance, standing with a wrapped gift in her hand.

It was Mia.

Christel's first instinct was to close her heart off from the encounter. She had hated Mia for so long for what she'd done to their family. In large part, Christel still held her responsible for her father's accident. The loss at her former best friend's hand had been immeasurable.

Christel was reminded of her brief conversation with Mia in the parking lot after meeting with Jay. She'd been foolish enough not to tell Evan she was meeting with her ex-husband, partly because of her conflicted feelings and the idea her former husband still held a spot in her heart.

What Mia had seen that day could have been twisted. Mia held the power to hurt her...yet she hadn't. Instead, she had promised to keep the meeting to herself and allow Christel the opportunity to tell Evan in her own time and in her own way. The gift had not been lost on Christel.

She'd been forced to evaluate the hatred she carried toward her former best friend. She'd opened her heart to the possibility that Mia was not the monster Christel formed her to be in her mind.

Christel had followed in the footsteps of her mother and Alani. She'd dropped her rocks, so to speak, and chosen to toss them aside, electing to extend forgiveness. While still fresh and weak, that forgiveness is what made her grant the woman standing across the lawn a timid smile.

That was all it took for Mia to begin walking in her direction.

Shane turned. "You coming?"

He noticed Mia.

"Uh...take your time." He glanced between the two women, assessing the situation. When he failed to see his sister's face contort with anger, he gave his head a simple nod. "I'll make sure they save you some pineapple cake." He gave her an encouraging smile before turning and picking up his pace in order to catch their mom, who was now several feet ahead of him.

Mia neared and held out a beautifully wrapped package. The oblong box was covered in paper printed with a pink and blue metallic floral design and tied with a matching ribbon. An expensive-looking linen envelope was tucked under the bow on top. "This is for you," Mia said.

Christel took the offered package and thanked her. "It's beautiful." Mia always loved giving presents, and the look in her eyes was reminiscent of many times before when she'd waited with anticipation as Christel opened one of her carefully wrapped packages.

Christel tucked the box under her arm and opened the envelope. Inside was an embossed card that read, "For my friend, Christel...and her babies."

The sentiment was simple yet filled with meaning.

Christel looked into Mia's face. "Thank you."

"Open it," Mia urged.

Christel grinned. This was so like her former best friend. "Okay, okay. Here, hold this." She handed off the card and envelope to Mia and set about the task of undoing the gift wrap without tearing it.

"Oh, just rip it!" Mia laughed.

Christel's heart warmed. "Don't get impatient."

The exchange felt like old times. Times before the grenade went off in all their souls.

Finally, the package was free of the wrapping. Christel let the paper drift to the ground as she focused on opening the box.

One quick peek and Christel's eyes filled with tears.

Inside, were the two handmade dolls they used to play with when they were little girls. Their *babies*.

The dolls were more ragged than she remembered but showed signs of being well-loved. Memories flooded as she looked into the eyes of her friend a second time. "Where did you get these?"

Mia smiled. "Mom had them tucked at the top of one of her closets. When she was fighting cancer, I spent time cleaning and found them." She bit at her lip. "I thought maybe your children might enjoy playing with them." She pointed. "There's a boy and a girl. So, it's perfect."

An emotion-filled tear wandered down Christel's cheek. "They're perfect. Thank you, Mia." She meant it. This was such a thoughtful gift, one that spoke volumes of the time they'd spent playing *mommy*...both little girls dreaming of that someday when they would be real mothers.

"I am so incredibly happy for you, Christel. You more than deserve all this happiness."

Somehow, the remaining hard feelings Christel had harbored melted, and all that remained was a strong desire to reconnect with this woman who knew all her childhood secrets and dreams.

She stepped forward and pulled her friend into an embrace.

"I've missed you," she whispered against Mia's long dark hair.

"I've missed you, too," Mia whispered back in a choked voice.

Christel wasn't sure how long they stood like that, holding onto each other.

Some people believe that without history, our lives amount to nothing. At some point, we all have to choose: do we fall back on what we know, or do we step forward to something new?

It was hard not to be haunted by the past. Their history was what shaped them...what guided them. All of it...good and bad.

No doubt, going forward, her history with Mia would resurface from time to time. When ugly memories reappeared, Christel would have to remember that sometimes the most important history was the history they were making today.

12

Aiden returned to the station after the luau, elated that his sister and brother-in-law now had the family they so badly wanted. He couldn't have written the end of that story any better. They were both wonderful people, and they deserved this happiness.

The Briscoes all believed that family was everything. Now, Christel had one of her own.

Smiling, he entered the station to find Jeremy Hogan storing a safety belt in one of the side cubbies on the rescue unit.

"Hey," he said. "How'd the family thing go?"

"Great!" Aiden patted his stomach. "I'm stuffed. If anyone went away hungry, it wasn't because of lack of food."

Jeremy nodded with a grin. "Yeah, no one puts on a better spread than Alani Kané. Te Au Kane luaus are famous."

"You both just like to eat," Meghan said, coming around the emergency vehicle. She playfully patted her co-worker on the stomach. "Especially you, Jeremy."

Out of everyone at the station, Jeremy struggled to stay within the station's mandated BMI limits. Aiden decided to join in on teasing him about it. "A little kalua pork isn't going to hurt. It's that bag of caramels you have stashed in the kitchen behind the stack of paper plates." He handed Jeremy the rappelling gear tangled at his feet.

"Ah, what...you found my goods?" Jeremy groaned. He straightened the gear and found a place for it inside the cubby. "Guess that means my special treat is all gone."

Meghan's elbow bumped him. "Nah, I got your back. I relocated your stash to the broom closet."

Jeremy broke into a wide grin. "Do you want to marry me?"

"Not on your life," was Meghan's quick retort. "My standards are far too high. Besides, have you smelled your empty boots lately?"

Laughing, she turned her gaze upon Aiden as she picked up a pair of bolt cutters and secured them in the empty spot next to the safety belt.

He could sense Meghan's body next to his, could feel her arm as it grazed his own.

He cleared his throat, hoping to clear his mind of stray thoughts. This girl had been taking up a lot of space in his head. Good or bad, it needed to stop.

She smiled at him as if reading his mind. "So, it's been quiet all morning. No incident reports."

"Good." Aiden stepped back and ran his hand through the top of his hair. "Downtime is good. Allows us to address the backlog of admin stacking up." He turned to Jeremy. "Did you get last week's reports cataloged?"

"I did." Meghan placed her hands on her hips. "And I filled out the requisites for that extra ladder and the axes we talked about in the meeting on Monday."

Jeremy closed the cubby. "Show off." He turned to face them. "Well, if we're racking up points, let it be noted that I cleaned the refrigerator. These people are pigs. Tossed something left in a bowl that I swear was growing."

Grant Costa came jogging down the metal steps from the offices on the second floor. "Hey, you're back."

Aiden nodded. "Yeah, sorry you guys had to cover for me this morning."

"No problem. It was quiet," Grant reported.

"That's what I was told." Aiden forced himself not to gaze over at Meghan. If he wanted his team to follow the rules, he couldn't be one to break them. His mentor, Captain Dennis, often told him before he'd retired that good leaders always show the way.

Just because he was doing the right thing didn't mean he was happy about not pursuing a relationship with Meghan. He'd worked alongside her long enough to grow to admire her spirit. She was the perfect complement to him. She didn't care what others thought. Meghan followed her heart.

Of course, she hadn't been the one promoted to captain. He had. His position came with responsibilities that couldn't simply be shirked off because some girl was making it hard to breathe.

If he could follow this feeling...well, a lot would be different.

Don't get him wrong; he'd dated. Each time he'd found a good reason to keep the relationships at arm's length. Sydney Alexander hadn't been the only aggressive girl he'd encountered.

There were ones who immediately wanted to take over and control his schedule...whom he spent time with, where he went and demanded to know why he hadn't texted or called every day.

Some were incessantly late. If you wanted to be somewhere at a particular time, you had to lie and tell them the reservation was at least an hour earlier than it actually was. Once, he'd sat in his car for over forty-five minutes waiting for his date even to get home. Then she had to take a shower. Time means nothing to some girls.

A couple of them were so into designer bags, shoes, and the latest trends in fashion that they spent their time at dinner with their heads buried, scrolling their favorite retail sites on their phone. He'd learned not even to try to have a meaningful discussion with those women.

He'd seen a girl named Rebecca a couple of years back. They got together infrequently because of the demands of both of their jobs, but when he did spend time with her, it was good. Eventually, she claimed the relationship had grown stagnant and recommended they go their separate ways. Sadly, by then, he barely cared about ending the relationship.

Shane often accused him of being too picky, but why settle? Why accept a level of misery just to be in a relationship with someone who was never meant to be your soul mate?

He was jumping ahead, but someday he'd like to find someone to share his life with. Think about it. He would no longer open the lock and push the door open to an empty house. He wouldn't be cooking ramen noodles and eating beans from a can because he didn't have the motivation to cook for himself. Why bother?

Last week, he'd opened the refrigerator and found empty shelves. Why shop when he couldn't eat the food before it expired?

It would be kind of nice to no longer eat alone most days. In fact, he wouldn't mind having someone to talk to when he'd had a hard day. Someone to cuddle with on the couch in front of a good movie with a bowl of popcorn.

All of his siblings had someone. Katie had a whole family to share her life with. In the past year, his mom met Tom, and Christel had married Evan and now had a daughter and son. Shane had become a different person after Carson. His little brother's cup was now full and overflowing—no lack there. Aiden was the only one hanging out there, feeling lonely.

Maybe he needed to get a dog.

Whom was he kidding? He was never home enough to care for an animal.

He snuck another look at Meghan.

Jeremy said something funny, and she was laughing. He loved Meghan's laugh, the way she put her whole self into the joy of it. She laughed easily. Life wasn't filled with serious obligations. She took life as it came and wrung all the happiness she could get from every experience. She was tough as nails and thrived on the thrill of adventure—she loved nothing more than capturing a situation and making it her own. On her terms.

She turned, and their gazes met.

A smile crept over her face as if she held a secret. One she couldn't wait to share with him.

Aiden could hear his own breath, feel his own heart beating against the bone in his chest. Just from that one intense look.

He had to do something...or he would be too weak to turn this around.

When he first started as captain, he had difficulty setting boundaries and expectations. He wanted everyone to like him. He wanted the people here to feel like they were part of a family because that is what the station had always been to him. Extended family. But it didn't work like that. He didn't need his team members to like him. He needed them to respect him and do their jobs well. Lives depended on that.

How could he maintain respect if they felt he was giving preference to one of the team because he was in a relationship with her? The manual made it clear—no fraternizing with those you manage—especially when concern for someone you love could possibly affect judgment and decisions in a crisis.

Turn a few pages, and he'd found another warning about

dating if one is a supervisor over another and the ethical issues that raised. One could tank or boost the career of the other. Coercion to have an unwanted intimate relationship in the workplace was a huge no-no; even the appearance of it being possible was strictly forbidden.

Bottom line?

This wasn't going to happen.

13

Ava looked up at the sound of a light rap on her office door. "Come in," she hollered as she straightened the stack of field inspections she'd been going through.

"Hey, there. Am I interrupting?"

Ava smiled upon seeing Tom at her doorway. "No, not at all. I'm glad to see you." She grinned. "Fact is, I was getting hungry. You want to wander over to the restaurant and see what Jon has on the menu?"

Tom held up a brown paper sack. "I thought you might say that. I took the liberty of grabbing us something."

Ava felt a familiar warmth spread over her. This is why she adored this man. Not only was he thoughtful, he often could anticipate her needs and made filling them his priority.

"You are a keeper," she announced, motioning for him to join her at the small round conference table by the windows overlooking the golf course they had built together. "And I'm glad you dropped by for another reason besides my empty stomach."

"Oh?" He pulled sandwiches from the bag and unwrapped them, pushing one in front of her.

She lifted the meat-filled hoagie bun and left it suspended a few inches from her mouth. "Yeah, I wanted to talk to you about something I've been concerned about."

He opened the small bag of chips that came with his meal. "What's up?"

Ava reached and covered his free hand with her own. "I know the Briscoes can be a bit much."

He dumped the chips onto the paper. "I'm not sure I'm following you."

"You took on a lot when you decided to make me a part of your life." And he had. Life at Pali Maui could be a circus at times, especially when you throw in the entire Briscoe bunch and their adventures. Tom had gotten much more than he had signed up for.

"I think we might want to plan a weekend getaway after the talent show—just the two of us. Go someplace romantic?" The look she gave him conveyed that she understood what she'd forced upon him.

Tom dropped his sandwich, stood, and circled the table. He took Ava by the hand and pulled her into his arms. "I am the happiest I've ever been," he whispered against her hair. "You are the first thing I think of when I wake and the last thing my mind sees before sleep." He paused and looked her in the face. "Please don't think your family and business obligations intrude on how I feel about you, Ava. This is you, your life—I love it all."

His words of reassurance melted her anxious heart.

Early in her marriage to Lincoln, there was a time when she thought he was her one true love. She never considered herself capable of loving anyone else...even after learning of his infidelity. They had married, raised babies, and nurtured Pali Maui into the island's premier pineapple grower. Yes, the effort for parenting and business had fallen primarily onto her shoulders, but he was still her partner in the effort...in life.

How is it, then, that she was so blessed to have met someone else? Tom Strobe was a marvelous man—caring, brilliant, so good-looking he would walk into a room, and her knees would quiver.

The best part? He cared deeply about her and offered her a stable relationship based on respect, trust...and love. Yes, she could admit it now. She'd fallen in love with Tom. The indications were that he felt the same.

Ava had learned a difficult lesson after losing Lincoln. Love was a gift, something to hold on to and nurture. No amount of letting a relationship coast was beneficial. She wanted desperately to make sure Tom was happy.

She took the sides of his tanned face in her hands. "I love you." She swallowed. There, she'd said it. The sentiment could never be repeated often enough.

"And I adore you," he told her. "More than you know."

Tom pressed his lips against her temple, then lowered his mouth to her lips. She inhaled the scent of him, put her arms around him, held him tight, and returned the kiss. He tilted his head, deepening the kiss. She opened her lips under his, satisfied with the deep moan that escaped him as he slid his hands down her back and pressed himself more solidly against her. This man was in shape.

She pulled away just slightly. "Is this a good idea?" she whispered. "I mean, we're at my office."

"Oh, yeah. Best idea I've had all day," he teased.

He kissed her again, deeply. She did not pull away. When Tom finally paused, she muttered, nearly breathless, "Maybe we should wait until we have more privacy."

"Okay," he said, going after her lips again.

They were like two college-aged kids with nothing to consider but their feelings and need for each other. When she was with Tom, she was no longer a mother, a grandmother. She was a girl in a bikini with a surfboard tucked under one arm, laughing and running for the water.

A horn honked. There was a distant sound of familiar laughter, now growing closer.

Ava groaned and dropped her head to Tom's chest. "I'm thinking of putting my kids up for adoption."

He laughed. "I don't think you can do that once they are over eighteen."

"Then I'm going to lock my doors and take away their keys."

That made him laugh even more. "As I said, Ava. It's a package deal. I love all of it."

"You might say that now. We'll see how you feel in a few years when there are more kids, more dogs, and more chaos."

She looked at him, knowing the future was hard to predict. Yet she knew this...she wanted her future to include Tom Strobe.

14

Jon dumped his remaining coffee into the sink and placed his empty mug on the counter.

"Don't forget to rinse the sink," Katie stood from the barstool at the island. "That copper basin cost a bucket of money, and I don't want it stained."

Jon patiently smiled at his wife and did as she asked, spraying water around the sink from their equally expensive designer faucet. She was a pain in the rear, but he loved her.

When he finished, he turned and pulled his wife, who was now standing a few feet away with her attention buried in her phone, into an embrace. "There. Better?"

Before she could answer, Willa came bounding out of her second-story bedroom and down the floating staircase. "You're taking me with you today, right, Dad?"

The school was closed for teacher in-service. He'd promised his daughter she could go to work with him. "Sure. Get your things."

Katie frowned. "You are going to work with Dad?"

Willa grabbed her backpack and slung the straps over her shoulder. "Yeah. He's going to teach me to bake a pineapple soufflé. That's considered master level. But I'm up for it. Kina and I plan to make things and auction them at the talent show. Pineapple soufflés will raise a lot of additional funds."

Katie raised her eyebrows. "So, we have another chef sprouting up in the family?"

Jon beamed. "Looks that way." He turned to his daughter. "Chefs' hours are early. We'd best get going."

He leaned over and whispered in Katie's ear. "I won't let her cross-contaminate this time."

She gave him a peck on the cheek and whispered back, "You say that, Jon...but you eat the soufflé first. If you don't get sick, I'll try some."

Oblivious to her parents' private conversation, Willa turned to her mother. "Bye, Mom."

Little Noelle was sitting on the floor playing with her Minnie Mouse doll. "Me come! Me come!" She stood and lifted her arms in their direction.

Jon kissed her head. "Not today, sweetheart. But Daddy and sissy will bring you home a cookie."

"Minnie, too?"

"Minnie, too," he assured her.

That seemed to satisfy her. She dropped back to the floor and picked up her fabric doll and patted her on the head. "Daddy will bring us a *tootie*."

Katie patted her husband on the back as he turned for the door. "Bribery will get you everywhere."

No Ka 'Oi was located on the Pali Maui property near the northern end of the newly renovated golf course and was within walking distance from Jon and Katie's house. The farm-to-market restaurant was Jon's brainchild and offered unique food selections that tempted even the most distinguished palate. Often, the reservation list was extended weeks out.

Jon and Willa entered the kitchen through the back door. Jon hung his jacket on the hooks lining the short hallway and extended his hand to his daughter, offering to store her backpack.

Before handing it over, Willa fished out her cell phone and tucked it into the pocket of a white apron she pulled from another hook. She put it on, tying the straps around her waist.

"Well, come on, sweetheart. We have a lot to do before the lunch crowd arrives."

Jon surveyed the activity in the kitchen. His sous chefs were all busy chopping and dicing fresh shallots and mushrooms. Another stirred a bowl filled with homemade red pepper sauce. "Hey, Jon. I was sure our delivery yesterday included a sack of garlic. This morning, there were only two bulbs left in the sack. Somebody use them?"

Jon shook his head. "Not that I know of."

Peka straightened his tall white toque and shrugged. "Oh, well. Add that to the list for tomorrow."

Jon nodded and waved for Willa to follow him into the pantry. "Grab that wire basket over against the wall and fill it with fresh pineapples," he told her. "We'll also need that bag of brown sugar."

Willa did as she was told. When she lifted the sack, what little remained of the brown sugar spilled onto the floor.

"Be careful!" Jon scolded.

"I didn't do it. There was a hole in the bottom of the sack."

Still trying to figure out how the sack got a hole, Jon grabbed the broom. "Look around for another sack while I clean this up."

Willa lifted on tippy-toes to the top shelf. "I think there's one up there." She grabbed the kitchen stool and retrieved it.

In the kitchen, they laid out all the ingredients...white sugar, eggs, butter, some slices of white bread, and brown sugar.

"I'll cut up the pineapple while you mix the other ingredients," Jon told her. "Use that big bowl."

"Dad? Which cupboard?"

Jon pointed.

He looked to see his reservation hostess, Maria, heading his way with a clipboard. A bright red hibiscus tucked behind one ear matched her flowing muumuu. "Hey, Jon. I think we've overbooked for lunch. The online system still seems to be glitching."

Jon wiped his hands and leaned over to peek at her list. "Ah, well...at least it's only one party. We can accommodate that. Set up another table near the breezeway."

She nodded. "That'll work."

A loud shriek drew both of their attention.

Willa screamed a second time and slammed the cupboard door. "Dad!!"

He rushed to her side. "What is it?"

"It's a...I don't know what it is. But it had teeth. Sharp pointy ones."

Jon scowled and reached for the cupboard door, easing it open. He was immediately met with a hiss. Before he could slam the door closed, the animal leaped forward and landed on the floor. The varmint scurried across the commercial linoleum and over Maria's open-toe heels.

She shrieked and threw her clipboard. The clipboard sailed through the air. On the way down, it hit the bowl of red sauce, flipping it into the air. Red, gooey sauce rained onto them all and splattered onto the floor.

"What was that?" Willa yelled. She stepped back and slipped. Her right leg went in one direction. Her other leg slid the opposite way. Before she could stop herself, she puddled onto the floor and the red sauce.

Jon moved to catch her. He, too, slid and went down.

"Ouch!" he yelled, feeling his wrist hit the floor.

Sitting on the floor in the puddle of red, Willa pulled her phone out and quickly shot off a text.

"What are you doing?" Jon asked, trying to lift himself.

"I texted Uncle Aiden."

"Why?" He felt himself slip again and grabbed the counter's edge to steady himself.

His hostess looked at him through red-speckled eyeglasses. "I think it was a mongoose."

"A what?"

Peka held his spoon at his side. He, too, was splattered with red. "A mongoose."

Jon impatiently scowled. "I heard what she said."

Peka shrugged. "You asked."

Jon groaned. His wrist was swelling. He looked around. "Let's get this kitchen cleaned up. We have a lunch crowd showing up in a couple of hours."

Maria gave Jon a sympathetic look to soften her warning. "If health inspectors show up, you won't want a mongoose in the kitchen."

"I know that," Jon said, slightly more sharply than he intended. "First things first. We have to clean up this mess."

It was an effort, but with the help of all the kitchen staff, Jon and Willa got the floor mopped and the cupboards wiped down. There were even a few spots on the ceiling. "Those can wait," Jon announced, finally sitting down to inspect his bruised wrist.

Peka peered over his shoulder. "Looks like you sprained it pretty good."

Jon didn't need to be told that bit of information. He knew he injured his wrist pretty badly when he slipped and went down. Sprains healed, but they were painful. He'd have to take a lot of aspirin and keep it wrapped for a few days.

"Hey, what's up?"

Jon looked over to see his brother-in-law entering the kitchen, followed by the girl that worked with him at the station. Was her name Meghan?

"Aiden. What are you doing here?"

Aiden hooked a thumb in Willa's direction. "I got a text."

Jon groaned. "Oh, man. I'm sorry. She shouldn't have—"

"But, Dad. Aiden can help us trap that mongoose. He's good at that kind of thing."

"He's got a job," Jon scolded. "Your uncle can't just drop everything and come deal with our problems."

Aiden waved off his concerns. "Eh, we're here. Let's see what we can do."

Jon hated to admit it, but Aiden's help was welcome.

Peka wiped his hands on a kitchen towel. "So, you're getting help from the big guns." He grinned.

Jon nodded in his brother-in-law's direction. "Well, one gun...but big enough."

15

Meghan followed Aiden to the back storage room. "So, I guess your brother-in-law discounts the really big gun in this duo." When he turned, she gave him a teasing look. "Fifty bucks says I trap that varmint before you do."

"I don't know. I appreciate the confidence, and I would never discount your ability, but we're likely talking about a mongoose here. Sharp teeth. You might get bitten."

Meghan pointed to some ten-pound sacks of flour leaning against the wall. Several had holes with flour piled on the floor. "Yup. They didn't chew through those bags with their gums."

"They?" Aiden lifted his eyebrows. "How do you know there's more than one?"

"Mongooses are highly social animals. Alpha males and their devoted females mate for life and are rarely seen apart. While small, they are excellent hunters with remarkable reflexes. They hunt mice, rats, rabbits, lizards, and snakes."

"Apparently, they also enjoy brown sugar and flour."

Meghan grinned. "Looks that way."

Aiden ran his hand across his neck. "How do we even know

they're still here? The open door might have invited them outside."

Meghan pointed to a high shelf. "I don't think so."

On the shelf, a mongoose peered from behind a sealed box of paper goods.

Meghan parked her hands on her hips. "Challenge on."

She pulled her cell phone out of the pocket of those tight jeans and scrolled across the tiny screen with her thumb. "Okay, got it." She pointed to a shelf on the opposite side of the room. "Close both doors, and I'll grab that water jug."

Aiden followed her directions. "So, what's the plan?"

"Get me a knife. We're going to cut the top off this jug like this." She held up her phone for his inspection.

He raised his eyebrows. "Might just work."

"It will work," she declared. "We got this."

Aiden loved her enthusiastic confidence. "We got this," he repeated.

It took nearly an hour to replicate the trap she'd found on the internet. When finished, they exchanged glances and said in unison, "We got this."

According to the information she'd pulled up, the key to trapping the intruders meant hiding the contraption they'd built with a lure inside...in this case, a tiny bowl filled with raw eggs. Meghan placed a small pile of raisins next to the bowl as an added incentive.

"Okay, I think we have it positioned just fine. Now, we need to wait."

"Did the article say how long it normally takes for the mongoose to check it out?"

Meghan shook her head. "No, but we got this."

The mantra brought a smile to both of their faces.

The mongooses were nowhere to be seen. Aiden motioned for Meghan to follow, and they headed for the kitchen, carefully closing the door behind them.

"Well?" Jon asked as he looked up from sliding Willa's soufflé inside the industrial oven. He set the timer.

Willa hoisted herself up onto the counter. "Did you catch it?"

Her father immediately told her to get down. "You can't sit on the food preparation surface, honey."

Aiden gave his niece a playful punch on the arm. "Yeah, goofball." He offered her a hand and helped her down, then watched as Jon sprayed disinfectant and wiped down the spot.

"There are at least two mongooses," he reported.

"Two?" Jon's face bloomed with exasperation. "Maybe more?"

"Maybe," Meghan told him. "But we saw two. It's only a matter of time, and we'll catch—"

Before she could finish her sentence, a commotion from the storage room drew their attention.

Aiden quickly moved to the door and placed his ear against it. "Sounds like we got 'em."

Meghan held up her hand. "Don't open it. Not yet."

She joined him at the door, and they both listened.

Aiden was acutely aware of her against him. The smell of her hair was intoxicating. Despite the racket on the other side of the door, his world stood still.

"What's going on?" Willa asked, leaning over nearby.

"Honey, get back," her father warned. "Stay out of their way."

The noise on the other side of the door quieted slightly. Aiden glanced back at them. "We're going in."

He looked to his partner-in-crime. She nodded in agreement.

Slowly, he eased the door open.

Across the room, two mongooses were crammed inside the clear plastic container, feasting on eggs and raisins. The trap door shut them inside.

A broad smile sprouted on Meghan's face. She slapped at Aiden's chest and held out an open palm. "Fifty bucks. Pay up."

Aiden sighed and went for his wallet.

"Better yet—" A smile crept over her face. "Take me to dinner."

His shaky breath filled with an acute sense of responsibility that wrestled with an impregnable desire to remain in her presence. In a moment of absolute weakness, he looked into her ocean-blue eyes and said, "Okay, sure."

16

Aiden stepped inside his shower and chastised himself. How could he let himself be so stupid?

He'd agreed to take Meghan McCord to dinner against his better judgment. Not exactly his best decision.

He positioned himself under the hot, streaming water, letting the flow beat against his back. Putting himself in a situation where he faced the chasm between what he wanted to do and what he should do was dancing with danger. As dedicated as he was to his duties as captain, his willpower did have a limit. Alcoholics shouldn't roam the liquor aisle at the store, and he shouldn't be going to dinner with Meghan.

He supposed he could use this opportunity to clarify their relationship and make it clear that a romantic bond could not be fostered. Yes, that's what he'd do...leave no room for the relationship to grow past the appropriate boundaries.

Meghan understood protocol. When he explained the situation, she'd realize that any feelings she might have for him would have to be placed on hold indefinitely.

Did she have feelings for him? He thought so. Every time she looked at him, he saw something in her eyes that expressed more than casual regard. More than once, she'd allowed her hand to linger on his arm. The signals were there...or at least he thought so.

Aiden squirted shampoo into his palm and rubbed it against his hair, scrubbing as if washing away the warm feeling building in his gut.

He closed his eyes and let her image surface. Meghan's delicate skin contradicted the strength of her sculptured forearms, stomach, and legs. Soft vs. hard. Jet black hair spotlighted the cool blue in her eyes.

The roaring physical impulse surprised him, and he slammed the water off and grabbed a towel. In the privacy of his mind, he entertained a flame that could burn him.

He had to stop.

Determined to do just that, Aiden stepped from the shower and looked in the mirror as he dried himself. Tonight...he'd definitely cut all this off. No matter his emotions, he'd build a wall between them that neither could traverse.

Leadership came at a price. He only wished the cost wasn't this high.

~

AIDEN ARRIVED at Meghan's doorstep at precisely four o'clock, the agreed-upon time. He'd thought the hour a little early for dinner, but she quickly brushed aside any protests. "Quit overthinking all this. You're paying off your debt. Just show up."

Her place was just a short distance from where he lived in Lāhainā, a mere ten-minute drive. The single-story house was painted green with white shutters at the windows. The yard consisted primarily of a concrete driveway. While neat, there were no flowers or outward adornments.

Aiden took a deep breath and lifted his hand to knock, reminding himself of what lay ahead and his determined plans to remove himself from the temptation that had haunted him. One way to douse a flame was to aim a firehose and throw water on it.

He needed to talk to Meghan about his concerns.

The door opened before he could knock. She stood there wearing tight white leggings and an oversized pink top with matching sports shoes. His eyebrows lifted. "Uh, wow."

"Oh, don't look at me like that."

"I wasn't...I mean, you look great." And she did. She looked amazing.

"I know this outfit might not be what you expected," she said. "There's been a change of plans."

"What change of plans?"

She bid him inside. "I know you don't easily go with the flow, but trust me. What I have planned will beat any dinner served on a stuffy linen-draped tablecloth."

How did she know he'd made reservations at one of the trendiest and upscale restaurants on the island? Was he that predictable?

He made a mental note to cancel in secret.

She pointed to the counter. "Grab that, will you?"

"This?" He pointed to a backpack crammed so full the zipper bulged. "Could you get this any heavier?" Aiden lifted the pack onto his shoulder. "I mean, what did you put in here?"

"Wimp." She turned and went for the small kitchen. The room was tidy and sparsely decorated. She lifted an RTIC cooler from the floor and turned to her black lab. "C'mon, Scotch."

"I take it we're not going inside any dining establishment?"

Meghan shook her head. "Nope. Like I told you...change of plans."

She bounded out the door with Scotch at her heels. At the bottom of the porch steps, she turned. "Well, are you coming?"

He scrambled to follow her, feeling the weight of the pack. "Aren't you going to lock up?"

"Nah, if somebody needs my stuff so badly they feel they need to steal it; they can have it."

"Let's take my rig. You can drive." She opened the back passenger door of her sky-blue Range Rover, loaded the cooler, then climbed into the front seat and waited for Scotch to jump inside. "C'mon, Aiden. We don't have all day."

"More like we don't have much day left," he mumbled as he entered her vehicle and started the engine. Her spontaneity was both attractive and unnerving.

He looked across the seat. "Well, where to?"

She grinned back at him. "Haleakalā."

17

Captain Jack arrived at the Dirty Monkey just before
happy hour. The street out front was lined with an
array of vehicles, most belonging to tourists. Jack
could tell by the rental plates. Amongst them were a few he
recognized.

The old green pickup with the missing tailgate belonged to
Smitty Truant. He lived in a rundown wooden house not far
from the Olivine Pools—an idyllic, yet remote area on the
southern tip of the island. Few knew that Smitty's bank
accounts were brimming with profits from a roadside fruit
stand perched on an ancient lava shelf. In a rare moment of
candor, Smitty confided he spiked his signature smoothies with
homemade rum—or in Smitty's words, hooch.

Jack headed for the door to the bar, appreciating the fact
that, in a world often tilting with every wave, some things
remained the same. The Dirty Monkey provided an anchor to
many who lived in Lāhainā, a home away from home.
Including him.

When Jack stepped inside, it took several seconds for his
eyes to adjust to the dim light. The first thing he saw was the

familiar shark jaw mounted on the wall behind the cash register. No beachside bar was complete without a menacing marine predator trophy on display.

"Hey, Mole." He waved to the balding bartender.

"Hey, Captain Jack," the man greeted. "Got your rum on the rocks waiting for you."

His favorite drink was Kōloa Rum, made from pure sugarcane and pristine rainwater from Mount Waiʻaleʻale on Kauaʻi, and twice distilled in vintage copper pots. Not top shelf but smooth as a baby's butt and much cheaper.

Jack looked toward the end of the long, wooden bar lined with stools. True enough, at the empty spot next to where Smitty sat, a glass perched on the bar was filled with ice and dark rum.

Jack chuckled and rubbed at the portion of his belly that peeked from his half-buttoned shirt and moved in that direction.

Halfway, he caught sight of a slightly familiar woman sitting alone at a small wooden table. She was staring at the old-fashioned jukebox with neon lighting and holding a wine glass.

"There he is!" Smitty stood and waved Jack over.

Jack waved back and headed that way, wandering past the bar where a few haggard-looking men sat on stools, nursing their drinks. One was playing solitaire on the bar. In the back, a couple of fishermen he recognized from down on the wharf were playing pool.

He made his way to the end of the varnished wooden bar where his buddy sat. Smitty rubbed at his chiseled chin, rough with growth, before pulling Jack into a brief embrace. "'Bout durn time, bud," he said, with a pat on the back.

Jack slid into the empty seat next to Smitty. "Yeah, my doctor recently told me to watch my drinking, so I hurried to a bar with a mirror." He pointed to the massive mirror covering the wall behind the bar. A convenient mirror, he thought, as he stole another glance at the woman who sat alone. Dang, did he know her from somewhere?

Smitty stood and nodded in the direction of the bathroom. "Well, gotta go water a horse. I'll be right back."

Jack took hold of his drink and pulled a long swig, rattled the ice and then finished it off. He waved to the bartender. "Hit me again, Mole."

Jack peered at his reflection in the mirror. And that of the woman.

Their gazes met. She waved. "Hey, Jack," she said, loud enough to hear over the ukulele music on the jukebox.

Jack gave her a quick nod. A pleased grin lifted the corner of his lips as he suddenly realized it was the woman from child protective services, the one who helped deliver the twins into Christel and Evan's hands.

"Careful of that one," Mole warned, his voice low, as he delivered the second glass of rum. "She's way out of your league."

She stood and headed in his direction. "This rounds on me," she said. She pointed to the empty spot on the other side of Jack. "Is this taken?"

"It is now," Jack offered, a grin sprouting above his white beard.

18

The road to Haleakalā Highway was proof that, on Maui, the shortest distance between two points was rarely a straight line. After seventeen winding miles, they finally arrived at the summit.

Aiden eased the Range Rover next to an empty tour bus and parked. "Well, this is it."

He had to admit he'd enjoyed the conversation with Meghan on the way up. They had talked a lot about work-related stuff...the upcoming diving training next week, the requisition he'd put in for a second emergency vehicle, and the need for a single-serve coffee maker in the kitchen.

"The coffee gets stale in that glass carafe," she'd told him. "I vote for a new Keurig with all those little individual K-cups. The guys and I decided we'd take up a donation, if necessary."

Something in the lilt of her voice made his heart beat a bit faster.

"No worries. We can finagle the budget somehow." He'd secretly foot the bill himself, if needed, just to please her.

Now, sitting in the car in the parking lot, their conversation turned to more personal matters. "So, tell me about your dad."

The question caught him off guard. Intimate topics always made him feel unsteady. "Uh, what do you want to know?"

"You never talk about him."

He hesitated. Talking about his dad wasn't his favorite subject, and for a good reason. "I loved him very much."

Meghan seemed to weigh the statement. "Why?"

Aiden's eyebrows lifted. "Why? Well, many reasons. Lincoln Briscoe was a good man. I have many great memories."

He smiled, recalling one of his favorites. He told Meghan about when his dad flew him to Washington for a Seattle Seahawks game. "My dad loved football. He told me some of the best leadership lessons could be learned on the field. For example, the need to know when to carry the ball and when to pass it off to someone else. My dad was a proponent of the need for teamwork. He was a huge people person with an outgoing personality. He believed that people rarely win on their own without the help of others."

"Ah, that explains a lot about how you got your leadership skills," she said. She pointed to the back seat. "You thirsty? I can grab a can of soda from the cooler."

"Nah, I'm good." Aiden adjusted the heater control on the dashboard to ward off the chill from the air at this altitude.

"Tell me more about your dad," Meghan urged. "I love to hear about him."

Aiden pondered this for a brief second. It'd been months since he'd let the accident and the aftermath back into his mind. Some things are better left on a mental shelf. Still, she had trusted him with the knowledge that she was a foster kid. For that reason, he found himself wanting to confide in her.

"Dad used to tell me his secrets—just me. Once, he confided that when Mom got mad at him, he'd tighten the pickle jar so she'd have to talk to him and ask for his help."

Meghan laughed. "Clever."

Aiden nodded. "I know, right?"

Several moments of silence passed before Aiden gathered the courage to continue. "I never knew until after he died that he had a big secret he never shared." He looked across the seat, wrestling between wanting to share and the need for his family junk to remain private.

Meghan seemed to read his mind. She reached across and covered his hand with her own.

The gesture filled him with reassurance. His dad's failings were not his own. Shame was not his burden to carry.

Their eyes met. "He was having an affair," Aiden admitted, swallowing against the pain those words still formed in his chest. "With a trusted person who was many years younger. Like Christel's age. In fact, Mia was Christel's best friend in high school and the daughter of my mom's dear friend."

"Oh." The ugliness of the admission seemed to leave Meghan without words.

He instantly wished he'd kept the details of his father's infidelity to himself. Admitting what their family had experienced —what he had endured—left him feeling naked and scrutinized. Oh, how he hated his father for this. He hated himself for revealing all of it to Meghan now. Talk about a downer!

"Thank you for telling me, Aiden," she said quietly. "That certainly explains why you rarely mention your dad."

"Yeah, it's one of those things I'd just rather not talk about."

"I'm so sorry I—"

"No, that's okay. It felt a little good to tell you. I mean, not good, exactly. But you know what I mean."

She nodded. "Yeah."

They sat in silence for a few minutes. "I have a secret," she admitted.

Aiden glanced her way. "Most people do. Something you want to share?"

A sly smile sprouted on her face. "I'm interested in a guy."

Aiden felt the wind leave his lungs. She romantically liked

someone? Like in, for real? How could he have misread and thought she was interested in him? Had his own infatuation blinded him to the possibility that his feelings were not reciprocated? "Yeah?" he forced himself to ask.

"Look, I'm not the sort to dance around things," Meghan told him. "So, let me be blunt."

Aiden held his breath, waiting for the punch he knew was about to hit his gut.

"You're the one I'm interested in."

She waited.

Aiden froze. Did he hear her correctly?

"Say what?"

Meghan laughed. "You heard me. I like you—I think about you all the time. Well, not as much as I think about football, but a lot," she teased. "For claiming not to dance around, I could trend on TikTok with the way I'm sidestepping in this conversation." She looked directly at him. "Aiden, let me say it straight. I want to explore having a relationship that goes beyond friendship. I see the way you look at me. I think you feel the same. Am I right?"

Aiden gripped the steering wheel, not sure how to respond. He knew what he wanted to say but didn't dare go there. Still, he couldn't bear to lie and tell her he felt nothing. He'd planned on clarifying things, and this was his open opportunity.

"Meghan, you are an amazing girl..." he began.

Meghan pushed her head against the back of the seat. "Oh, no...not the 'you're an amazing girl' response."

Aiden drummed his thumb against the steering wheel. "No, wait. It's not what you think."

"What is it?"

"I do like you." There, he admitted it. The look on her face filled him with satisfaction. She was pleased to know her feelings were not solitary. She was happy he considered her in a romantic way beyond their working relationship. "I like you a lot."

"And?"

Okay, this is where the conversation would get complicated. "I am the captain down at the station, your boss."

Her head tilted slightly; her expression now confused. "Uh, yeah. I'm aware."

Aiden swallowed painfully. "We can't have that kind of relationship, Meghan."

"Why not?"

Aiden carefully explained the rules in place and why they existed. "I may not agree with not fraternizing with people who report to me, especially on a romantic level, but I understand why relationships of that nature are discouraged...especially in our line of work. Just imagine if we encountered a dangerous situation that I deemed might put you in harm's way. I may not want to, but unintentionally, I might hold you back and send someone else into the risk. Is that fair? No," he answered his own question. "There's no escaping that allowing my feelings for you to grow would affect my judgment in the field. I can't allow that."

Meghan stared at the floor of the SUV solemnly without speaking. Suddenly, she lifted her head and punched his arm. "Lighten up. We'll figure out something."

He loved her enthusiasm, but he was afraid he still needed to dampen the notion that they could move forward romantically. "Let's agree to be friends, for now. Good friends."

"Friends, huh? Well, I get to be the one who's a bad influence." She laughed.

"What does that mean?"

Her eyes twinkled with mischief. "You'll see."

She got out of the car and called the dog. "C'mon Scotch."

As they gathered the cooler, blanket, and coats she'd stuffed in her car, Aiden was surprised to see Meghan wearing a bright smile. Either she didn't feel the loss as intensely as he did, or she could pivot more easily—or, both. Either way, Aiden was glad the hard conversation was behind them. Any feelings they had for one another would remain fenced in and remain at a friendship level.

"Here, you grab us a good spot away from the crowd and spread the blanket," Meghan said. "I'll go get my telescope."

Aiden arranged their spot a short five-minute walk from where they parked. He was acutely aware of Meghan's presence as she joined him on the edge of the Leleiwi Overlook.

He'd done the right thing...said the right thing. Inside, he was still thinking all the wrong things. Like how great she looked and smelled. Fresh and clean, with a hint of trouble.

Pushing those thoughts from his head, he turned his attention to the view.

Most people blow right by in their frenzy to get to the summit, assuming that Leleiwi gives them another nice panorama down the mountain to the coast. Too bad, because the lava rim holds a surprise when suddenly the crater itself explodes into view.

"Would you rather go on to Kalahaku Overlook?" he asked, taking in the scene before him.

"No, that's where all the tourists gather. This is better."

Aiden watched as she expertly set up her telescope, aiming it toward the sky and making adjustments to the lens. He spread the blanket and put on the extra layers of clothing and coats. Temperatures would soon drop significantly as the sun went down.

Satisfied with the telescope, Meghan settled onto the blanket and opened the cooler. "I'm not much of a cook," she admitted. "But I know where to buy all the best food." She pulled out several containers labeled The Market Maui, a popular deli located in Wailea.

She handed him a wrapped sandwich. "This is a Ha'ole

Hoagie, made with sliced turkey, provolone, pickled onion, avocado, and greens, with some cumin aioli and mustard on the best sourdough you'll ever eat."

He took the sandwich. "My favorite."

"Really?" Meghan pulled a wine bottle from the cooler and two plastic stemmed glasses. She handed him the bottle and a corkscrew.

"Yeah, I eat there a lot. Amazing food." He uncorked the bottle and poured. "Let's see if that rings true for this cabernet as well."

The sky darkened as they ate. Clouds raced by and formed what looked like a quilt, waving in the sky below where they sat. Despite the lack of vegetation at this level, the air was filled with the scent of plumeria and 'ahinahina, a plant unique to Hawai'i that looked like plumes of feathers covered in thick, silver "hairs."

It wasn't long before the crowd perched on the adjacent overlook let out a vocal chorus of *"awe"* and *"amazing"* as the clouds broke the majestic skyline filled with orange, yellow and red. It was as if God Himself had picked up a brush and painted the horizon.

Aiden and Meghan sat quietly taking it all in.

As the colors began to fade, Aiden grabbed his glass of wine and took a sip. "That just never gets old."

It was then that he noticed Meghan's eyes. They were filled with emotion, so much so that they glistened with tears.

"The world is a beautiful place," she said in hushed tones.

In the distance, the crowd of tourists started to head back to their cars and tour buses. Aiden gathered up the remains of their meal and took the trash to a nearby receptacle. Meghan continued to sit, staring out at the sky.

"You okay," he asked upon returning.

"Huh? Oh, yeah. I'm fine," she assured. "I'm always taken by how lucky we are to live on this island, you know?" She turned to him. "I never want to take any of this for granted."

She hopped up and pointed into the darkening sky. "Look! I can already spot the Lepus Globular star cluster." She pointed. "See that?"

Aiden followed and spotted the celestial cluster. "Wow!"

"You think that's great, come look through the telescope."

Over the next hours, she pointed out amazing nebulae, constellations, and even a couple of, what she called, asterisms. "There's Orion and Aquarius. Oh, and over there to the far right is Delphinus, a well-defined rhombus of stars also known as Job's Coffin."

Aiden glanced around and realized they were nearly the only people left up on the ridge. He looked over at Meghan, fascinated by her knowledge of the night skies and how thrilled she became when talking about the galaxies and the cosmos.

"What are you staring at?"

He swallowed, embarrassed that he'd been caught. "Nothing," he lied. Then, feeling like an eight-year-old boy denying he'd brought a dirty frog into his mother's kitchen, he rubbed the back of his head and came clean. "Well, not nothing. I—"

Before he could speak another word, Meghan was beside him. She trailed a finger over his bicep and down his arm, slowly circling his palm with her thumb.

"Meghan—" He started to protest, but she placed a finger against his lips.

"Shh...don't. I heard you earlier. We're friends. Friends with obstacles. Yet, friends, nonetheless. Very good friends."

The air eased from Aiden's lungs as he felt the shift of her body and her lips met his own. His chest expanded and released with a heavy draw of air as thoughts of his dad pelted his brain. This must've been what it was like to know what you were doing was wrong, but there was no stopping.

As if under a spell, his gaze was drawn to her lips, parted

and full, and the sound of her shallow breathing filled him with a fierce longing. "Oh, Meghan," he whispered, with no power over the pull he was suddenly feeling.

In slow motion, he bent toward her, closing his eyes to caress her mouth with his own. A weak gasp escaped her as she melted against him. The sweet taste of her lips was far more than he bargained for, and he drew her close. With a fierce hold, he cupped the back of her neck and kissed her deeply, gently, possessive in his touch. His fingers twined in her hair, desperate to explore.

Her body melded to his with bold intensity. He was shocked when her mouth rivaled his with equal demand. He wanted more. Wanted—

With a heated shudder, he gripped her arms and pushed her back, his breathing ragged as he held her at bay. "We can't do this," he whispered. He dropped his hold and exhaled, running shaky fingers through his disheveled hair.

He returned his gaze to her face, riddled with regret. "Believe me, Meghan, as much as I want this, we can't."

She stared at him through glazed eyes and lifted her hands, taking both sides of his face in her palms. "That's where we differ, you and me. You see the world lined with fences, Aiden. I see wide open skies filled with dazzling stars."

Meghan brushed a sisterly kiss against his cheek, then pulled back and motioned between them. "And this? Well—" She grinned. "Never say never."

19

A va pulled the heavy-draped curtains back to catch a peek at the crowd. She turned to Christel. "Looks like a full house tonight."

Every seat was filled. At the back of the room, Willa and her best friend, Kina, stood behind a table with pleased looks on their faces as they sold their culinary goods to a line of people waiting with cash in their hands.

Christel stretched on her tiptoes to get a look over her mother's shoulder. "That's wonderful. Ori will be so pleased." She spotted Evan sitting next to Mig and Wimberly Ann in the second row. He held their sleeping babies in his arms. Christel wiggled her fingers in his direction, and he smiled back at her.

A vocal huff from behind drew their attention. Alani stood with her hands parked on her wide hips. "Ori might be pleased, but my son did not do this alone. A lot of volunteers and helpers stepped up and offered hours of time to this charity event." She clapped twice. "But enough chattering. Time for the show."

Ava and Christel exchanged amused glances. Their Alani was back. The cancer had not robbed her of her bossy nature.

They hastened backstage to join the rest of the cast.

All of Ava's kids were gathered. She felt a little guilty about pressuring them into performing, but coercing their involvement was justified. The storms on Maui had hit residents hard, and many were having difficulty getting back on their feet.

Ava was lucky and had insurance that rebuilt washed-away structures and restored the golf course at Pali Maui. Others were not so fortunate. Some businesses were barely reopening even now after all these months. Others had lost their homes.

Ori's brainchild, Ka Hale A Ke Ola Resource Center, had provided shelter, clothing, and food to hundreds, which left the center's resources at an all-time low—which is where this benefit came in.

Ava linked her arm with Tom's. "It's remarkable what Ori has accomplished in his thirty-four years. Even as a kid, Alani's son had a heart for helping others. When he was about ten, he announced he'd sold his prized baseball card. When Alani asked him why on earth would he do that, he shrugged in response and told her the local animal shelter was running low on food. 'Fifty dollars buys a lot of kibble, Mom,' he told her."

Tom pulled a water bottle from his lips and screwed the top back on. "Wow. No kidding?"

Ava nodded. "None of us were surprised when Ori decided to follow that same path as an adult and made helping others his vocation."

Alani checked her clipboard and waved a couple of silent instructions to the stage crew.

Tom checked his wristwatch. "Almost start time. And, by the looks of that crowd out there, this talent show will help provide services for some time."

Ori gave all of them waiting in the side wings a silent thumbs up. With a wide smile, he headed for the front of the makeshift stage and nodded. The curtains opened, and a round of applause rang out.

"Welcome, everyone. We are so pleased to have you with us tonight."

A slight case of nerves developed as Tom slipped his hand inside her own. Their act was his idea. She hoped the audience would find the presentation as humorous as she'd found the notion when he first mentioned it.

Her dead husband, Lincoln, would never—and that meant *never*—agree to look foolish, even for a good cause. She loved that Tom often set aside his pride and refused to take himself too seriously. That was only one of many things she adored about this man. Mostly, he made her feel like no one on the earth mattered more to him than her. One look and her spirits lifted. She felt cherished.

"Without further ado, please help me welcome our first act —ventriloquist Tom Sawyer and his dummy, Becky Thatcher!"

More applause came.

Tom grinned in her direction and led her onto the center of the stage, where a single ladderback chair now stood in the middle. He sat and pulled her onto his lap before arranging her flouncy blue skirt across her legs.

Ava did her best to mimic the wooden expression from their practice sessions. When Tom looked at her, she nearly broke character and had to bite her lip to keep from laughing, especially when she heard Mig chuckling loudly from the audience.

"So, Becky. Say hello to the audience," Tom instructed.

Ava's voice rang out, "Hello." At the same time, Tom acted as though he mouthed the word from behind his closed lips.

They did a whole routine like this. At the end of the act, Tom did something they hadn't practiced before the show. He lifted her to a standing position and kissed her right there in front of everyone.

Cheers rang up from the crowd.

Ava playfully slapped his shoulder, then together, they took a bow in unison and ran from the stage.

Next up were Katie and Jon. Jon was dressed in a suit and tie. Katie wore a pale-yellow dress with a full petticoat, making the skirt stand out. Christel followed them onto the stage, also dressed in a suit.

"Hello, everyone. I'm Lawrence Welk. This is Bobby and Cissy, and they will dance for you tonight."

Again, the audience broke into thunderous applause— especially the older generation who had grown up watching the Champagne Music Makers on television in the sixties. Right on cue, a bubble maker blew masses of tiny soap bubbles onto the stage and a jazzy tune began. Jon and Katie, aka Bobby and Cissy, waltzed around the stage while Christel bobbed a baton in the air to the beat of the music.

Two of Ori's friends showed up next, both dressed like Elvis. Their hips undulated to the tune "Hound Dog."

Backstage, Tom leaned toward Ava. "They aren't half bad."

"I know, right?"

A magic act was performed by the meat department manager down at the grocery store in Pukalani. His sleight of hand was fascinating...until he accidentally dropped one of the cups on the floor and had to retrieve it.

Ava could again hear Mig laughing loudly from the audience.

After a short intermission, several girls who ran the Banana Patch did an act where they all performed a gymnastic number that included cartwheels and handstands. One of the girls accidentally turned in the wrong direction and caused a couple of their co-performers to tumble to the ground. They laughed and recovered from the mishap by wagging their fingers at the culprit and pretending it was done on purpose.

"Good save," whispered Christel.

Then, it was Aiden and Shane's turn. As Shane passed Ava,

he grinned. "Make no mistake, Mom. We're going to get even for this."

As suggested by Ava, they took to the stage wearing long caftans with a seventies-style print and open sandals. Long wigs and round glasses topped off their Carole King look as they lip-synched the infamous song "I Feel the Earth Move." At the same time, some props aided in shaking the stage. The movement was significant enough to cause Shane's wig to shift. His hand quickly remedied the problem, but not before his dress split, leaving his bare back exposed above the waist. Going with it, Shane moved his hips in a circle and enjoyed as the audience howled with laughter.

Katie couldn't hold back her own laughter. She turned to her mom and sister. "Who knew Shane was such a goofball?"

Ava and Christel nodded simultaneously. "We did."

Their segment was at a close, and the two brothers went in for a bow. At the same time, Aiden's work phone buzzed, signaling an emergency alert. He dug into the dress pocket and pulled it out.

The expression on his face immediately changed, and he turned and ran off stage.

"Aiden, what is it?" Ava asked.

"An unexploded bomb, likely left over from World War II, was discovered by a couple of kids in an old sugarcane field."

20

B arely slowing, Aiden turned off the paved highway and onto the dirt road leading to the flatland known as the valley. His vehicle careened and sent loose red dirt flying. He pressed the gas pedal and gunned the motor again, heading in the direction of the flashing emergency vehicle lights in the distance.

The radio on his dashboard squawked. "Sight secured."

Aiden had little to do but think on the way here. Anyone living on the island was well aware of the history. The bombing of Pearl Harbor was decades ago, and memories of that time still rang in the minds of the senior citizens, many of whom were children at the time.

He remembered field trips to the memorial site on O'ahu and learning of the dreadful events of that December—a day said to live in infamy, according to FDR, the president of the United States at the time.

Aiden was also aware of the controversy over plans to detonate two stray bombs found in the waters near Molokini. He was in high school when protestors from around the world gathered and made the argument that, while making the reef safer for tourists, exploding a bomb underwater would have a devastating impact on marine life for decades to come. Ultimately, a decision was made to leave the munitions in place.

Most of the guys at the station still had mixed feelings about the remaining risk. Yet, the risk was manageable, given the deep-water location and the unlikely possibility of a diver being harmed.

This discovery posed a much different scenario—and far more dangerous. An undetonated military ordnance in an open field exposed anyone stumbling upon the bomb to an unintended explosion. The consequences could be severe.

He braked to a stop, threw open the door and ran over to Grant Costa. "What have we got?"

"A couple of boys were riding bikes in the old sugarcane fields. They built a makeshift ramp to use as a jump and that's when they came upon a rusty cylinder."

"Thank goodness they were smart enough not to mess with it." Aiden headed in the direction of multiple emergency vehicles, red lights flashing.

His team member ran alongside him. "The Army's Explosive Ordnance Division has been notified. They're on their way."

"ETA?"

"Should be anytime," Grant reported.

Aiden slowed as he neared the site. "Where are the kids?"

Grant pointed to a sheriff's car, parked a safe distance away. Two boys stood nearby. "We've cleared the area and secured the perimeter. The children's parents are on their way. From what we've learned, these fields were a military training site in the days following Pearl Harbor. All of Maui thought the island was next in line for an attack. Facilities were immediately erected, including live grenade courses, machine gun ranges, a bazooka area, a mortar and artillery impact area, and combat firing ranges for tanks. Amphibious training activities stretched from Māʻalaea Bay to Makena Landing."

"Got it. Until a few years ago, this land was filled with machinery and field workers. Why wasn't the bomb found earlier?"

Grant shook his head. "No idea. Guess the cylinder was covered by dirt and, later, by sugar cane stalks."

Aiden and Grant approached a group of men standing in a circle. He recognized a couple of the guys from the sheriff's office and nodded in that direction. One was on his handheld radio.

"Do we know if there are others?" Aiden asked, knowing the answer could dictate their approach.

A man wearing heavy army-green Kevlar body armor with a thick black chest plate and a helmet slipped his protection face shield up. "Dick Cloudt, EOD Officer." He removed a glove and extended his hand. "From the Explosive Ordnance Detonation unit."

"Captain Aiden Briscoe with the Maui Emergency Services. Our team stands by, ready to assist in whatever way needed." Like most in his profession, Aiden appreciated the adrenaline rush experienced in an emergency. He was glad this one was on someone else's shoulders. Tackling an undetonated bomb was too close to the boat explosion he'd been through. Not something he'd like to repeat anytime soon.

The EOD officer gave Aiden the rundown. "What we have is a single rusted cylindrical ordnance approximately two feet long and six inches wide, likely an aerial device. A small one compared to today's standards. This area hosted a military base during World War II."

"I'm surprised the bomb wasn't found earlier."

The officer shrugged and repeated what he'd already learned from Grant. "It's highly rare, but these things can be buried for years. That storm on Maui likely caused a rush of water that moved the earth and brought the unit to the surface. Frankly, we're lucky the thing didn't detonate at that time, given the possibility of it being jostled around."

The officer's radio squawked. He lifted it from its sheath on his chest and pressed the button. "Cloudt here." The voice on the other end reported that they were ready.

"Well, time for the big show. They have the trench built and are ready to set it off." The officer wiped sweat from his brow, then donned his helmet. He lifted his arm and gave a wave to the rest of his team members before heading in the bomb's direction.

Several other men from the Explosive Ordnance Detonation unit scrambled into place, some of them placing orange cones in a wide circumference. "Back. Get back!" They motioned for all of them to clear the area.

A car pulled up behind Aiden and Grant, and out jumped a woman with a panicked look. A man scrambled to follow her. "I'm the mom," she screamed. "Where's my Joey?"

"I'm here, Mom!" A kid in a Jurassic Park T-shirt and surfer shorts ran to meet his parents, pushing his bicycle past a stand of palm trees. Another kid followed. "We were just playing around, Mom."

He dropped the bike to the ground, and she pulled him into her arms.

"You're not in trouble," the man assured his son. He motioned for the second kid, and his arms went around his shoulders in a tight hug. "We're just glad you're both safe."

With the situation under control, Aiden glanced around. He spotted nearly all of his team members but one. "Where's Meghan?"

Jeremy wiped some fingerprints from his aviators. "She's back at the station."

Aiden frowned. "What is she doing back there?"

"She's packing up her office."

"What?" Aiden's chest immediately squeezed with anxiety. "Why is she packing her office?"

Jeremy shrugged. "I heard she quit."

A loud explosion sounded in the distance. The earth reverberated beneath Aiden's feet as a plume of thick, gray smoke lifted into the air.

"All clear!" someone shouted through a bullhorn.

He let out a sigh of relief. The bomb had been safely detonated. No one was hurt in the process.

Aiden gave a quick thumbs up to his team, then turned and ran for his vehicle. He had to get back to the office. Another bomb of a different sort had exploded...this time involving Meghan.

21

A va scanned the crowd for Tom. Finding him standing at Willa and Kina's table, she sidled up next to him as he handed a twenty-dollar bill to Willa in exchange for a coconut crème puff drizzled with chocolate. "Keep the change," he told her granddaughter.

"Thanks, Tom!" she told him with a wide grin.

"The funds go to a good cause," Kina reminded.

Ava smiled across the table at the girls. "So, how much have you girls made?"

Nearly in unison, Willa and Kina quickly reported, "Hundreds."

"Four hundred, to be more exact," Willa clarified.

"And forty dollars. Four hundred forty dollars at last count." Kina held up a wad of bills. "We've even had repeat customers."

Willa handed Tom a napkin. "Yeah, we're nearly sold out!"

Ava lifted the crème puff out of Tom's hand and took a sample bite. "Yum. I can see why."

Tom nudged her with his elbow. "Hey, get your own," he teased.

Willa lifted her open hands. "Grammy Ava can't. You bought the last one."

Responding to Ava's sad puppy eyes, he gave in. "Okay, fine...you can have it." He handed over the treat.

Ava didn't think twice. She took the offer and gave him a peck on the cheek. "Thanks. You're a keeper."

Tom glanced back at the girls. "Well, I should hope so. Few men would relinquish his dibs on a coconut crème puff."

"Homemade crème puff," Willa reminded.

A family of four approached the table. "Are we too late?" asked the mom.

Kina quickly shook her head. "Not at all. We still have kalua pork sandwiches and lots of cookies."

Tom linked his arm with Ava's. "So, any word?"

"No, and I'm anxious to hear."

"Aiden will text when he can," Tom assured her.

Katie and Christel approached. "Any word, Mom?"

"None." She shook her head. "I can't even describe what it's taking for me not to head out to the car and turn the radio on."

"Already did," Shane said, joining them. "Apparently, the bomb was safely detonated."

Relief rushed through Ava. "Oh, thank God. No one was hurt?"

"Not according to the radio report."

Christel pulled her phone from her pants pocket. "I'll text Aiden and check on things."

Jon joined them, still wearing his dancing costume. "What are you hearing?"

Katie turned to her husband. "The bomb was set off with no one hurt."

Jon adjusted Noelle on his hip. "Good to hear." He turned to his toddler daughter. "Are you hungry, baby?"

Her little dimpled finger went to her lips as if she was thinking this over. "I want a steak."

Willa laughed. "We don't have any steak, Noelle. How about a cookie."

Her little sister's face brightened. "Oh-tay!"

Ori threaded his way around several people and headed in their direction. He repeated the question they all had voiced. They assured him Aiden was safe and that the discovered bomb had not caused harm.

"Good," he said. "Hey, I can't thank you all enough for helping out today. Mom just told me they aren't done counting, but it appears we raised nearly thirty thousand dollars. That will go a long way in supporting the center and the people we serve."

Ava was shocked at the amount. "Thirty thousand? Wow!"

Alani sidled up and joined the conversation. "Based on the fact ticket sales could never equate to that much, I strongly suspect someone weaseled a donation into the mix."

All eyes shifted to Tom.

"What?" he said, squeezing Ava's hand.

Ava leaned her head against Tom's shoulder. "Yeah, I wonder who?"

∼

AIDEN TOOK the stairs two at a time. At the top, he darted for the last office door on the left—the door leading to his former office that now belonged to Meghan. Or, at least, it was hers.

Breathless, he reached the open door and peered inside. Meghan stood on the credenza with a hammer in her hand, using the back to unwedge some nails from the wall where her framed EMT license once hung.

"Meghan, what are you doing?"

She turned. "Hey, heard you had a big day."

"Cut the crap, Meghan. What is all this?" He motioned to the stack of boxes.

A slow grin formed on her face. "Hmm...all this is evidence I've resigned." She climbed down, picked up a sealed envelope off the desk, and pressed it into his hand. "I quit."

Aiden's heart thudded against his chest wall. "You can't quit."

Her eyes widened. "Can't? Who says?"

Without measuring his words, he blurted, "I'm your captain. Don't you think I should have been the first to know your intentions? It's protocol to—"

Without breaking eye contact, Meghan sauntered in his direction until she stood directly in front of him. "You are no longer my captain."

She held his gaze for just a little too long, and looked at him just a little too intently. Meghan then lifted on her toes, took his cheeks in both her hands, and brought her lips to his own.

Aiden pulled back slightly. "But—"

"Shh..." She kissed him again, this time with more intensity. Her lips were soft and tasted like raspberries.

Aiden couldn't help himself. He gave into her kiss, hungrily accepting all that it offered.

The urgency with which she kissed him was reciprocated. Warmth started in his toes and filled him until every cell of his body was aware of nothing else but her.

Her hair.

Her skin.

The way she smelled and tasted.

Right now, she could lead him into hell, and he'd gladly follow.

Finally, Meghan released him. She stepped back and silently studied his face. "So, aren't you going to open it?"

"Open what?" he stuttered.

She pointed. "The envelope."

Only then did he realize he still held onto what she'd placed in his hand.

Choking back and fighting to regain control, his hands shook as he slid a thumb under the seal, still damp.

Aiden pulled a single sheet from inside the envelop and opened it up.

"I hereby tender my resignation from the Maui Emergency Services Agency effective immediately. Signed—Meghan McCord." The document was dated that day.

"I don't understand," Aiden muttered. "You can't give up your career." Secretly, he mourned the idea of not seeing her every day.

"I didn't," she stated with her hands now on her hips. Her tiger tattoo seemed to be snarling at him. "We'll still be working together. I've taken a position with Airborne Aviation Utility, an agency that—"

"I know what they do."

"Then you know that we'll continue our rescue missions together. Our agencies will work in tandem, and our professional efforts will remain united...except for one very important thing. You will no longer be my boss and no longer face decisions that could be contrary to protocol and your responsibilities."

Her face broke into a wide grin. "I told you I'd fix this."

Aiden stood still, stunned and let the revelation sink into his conscience.

"This is where you are supposed to be happy," she urged. "Problem solved. Besides, I think I'll make a very hot helicopter pilot, don't you?"

"I can't argue that." He briefly closed his eyes, taking it all in. He didn't know if he'd ever felt more for a woman.

Meghan McCord showed up at the station all those months ago, a threat to his own career. At least in his mind.

She'd proven over and over that was not the case. At every turn, this tough, layered woman had put him first. He wouldn't want to cross her—she could be daunting—but he did savor the idea of spending time with her. Lots of time.

He wanted to know her at a deep and intimate level—to learn what made her secretly happy, what caused worry to mount inside her, what made her fear. He wanted to be the one who protected her and shielded her from all the hard things in life. Aiden desired to journey at her side and make her feel cherished, no matter what came.

He hoped to close his eyes with her next to him, to wake beside her and fight over who got the shower first. The future and possibilities were endless.

No more conflicted feelings. No uncertainty.

Aiden pulled Meghan into an embrace. "I was so scared I'd lose you," he admitted. "I was capsizing knowing you were leaving the station. Worrying I'd lose the greatest thing that has ever happened to me."

"You didn't lose me," she assured him. "I'm here. I'm right here."

They kissed again, this time, the touch of their lips was filled with promise, a future.

One thing couldn't be denied.

For the first time in his life, he was in love.

22

Katie picked up a candle from the store shelf, opened the lid from the jar, and brought the container to her nose, savoring the familiar fragrance. Tropical-scented items were abundant here on Maui and a tourist favorite. While perhaps overdone, the fragrant floral smell of plumeria remained one of her personal favorites.

She replaced the lid and put the item in her basket, then moved down the aisle, sampling several more while enjoying the fact that her myriad duties were not demanding her time.

She'd slipped away today to claim a little time for herself. Between managing the gift shop and the tours at Pali Maui, along with keeping a family and household in check, she'd found it harder to squeeze out an occasion where she could indulge her favorite pastime—shopping.

Katie couldn't wait to check out this new boutique in the Shops of Wailea. She'd met and chatted earlier with the owner, who had relocated from Los Angeles and brought a metropolitan flair to the items she offered for sale.

For example, instead of the common loose-fitting linens in bright pinks, blues, and greens found in most island stores, the clothing rack at Poppy Petals was loaded with trendy halter tops with large bow ties and figure-hugging pants in rich earthy colors. She tried on a top that looked like it'd been dipped in Hershey's chocolate and swooned. The shade complemented her complexion and looked rich and exclusive. Of course, she had to have it.

The brushed gold flatware in the dinnerware section also grabbed her attention, and she slipped a set of dessert spoons into her cart, not even bothering to look at the price. She'd likely have to sneak the purchase into the house without Jon seeing. He was always on her, teasing her about her inability to stay within her established budget.

It was the game they played—her husband would see something and ask if it was new. She'd answer, "That? I've had it for a while." Then, they'd exchange glances, a non-verbal acknowledgment of the truth.

Once, he'd tried to push the idea that she'd been buying too many shoes. She'd opened the spice cabinet door and pointed. "Want to compare, babe?"

Katie smiled at the memory as she wheeled her cart to the register.

A tall woman, who was impeccably dressed, smiled at her. "I hope you found everything you were looking for."

"And then some," Katie said, opening her purse. She was in the process of paying when her phone rang.

She pulled her cell from her purse and lifted it to her ear. "Hey, Christel. What's up?"

"I was up all night, that's what. Why didn't you tell me that having infants meant never sleeping, taking a shower, or combing your hair? I didn't even brush my teeth this morning."

"You sound cranky."

"I am cranky. You would be too if you were covered in throw-up and smelled."

"Welcome to motherhood," Katie told her, pulling her

credit card from her wallet. She smiled at the lady standing across the counter from her.

Christel's voice softened. "Even with all that...it's wonderful."

"I know, right?" Katie pressed her security code into the point-of-sale machine. "No one can describe the wonder of it all...especially when they lay their tiny heads against your chest, and you feel their warm breath on your skin."

Her sister sighed on the other end of the line. "I know. It's amazing. I'm not complaining, but I feel like I lost myself between the bottle feedings and the six dozen diapers I changed yesterday."

"You need sex." Katie looked up to see the store clerk suppressing a smile. Katie winked at her and continued. "I mean it; you need some time in sweaty, tangled sheets. Let me come over and babysit."

"Sex is the last thing on my mind," Christel argued.

"Which is why you need some *bedtime bingo* pronto."

Katie thanked the clerk, gathered her bag of purchases, and headed out the door. Several yards away, she saw a familiar figure enter the store next door. Curious, she walked in that direction until she could glance up at the signage above the entrance.

When she did, she gasped. "Christel, hold on a minute."

"What's going on?"

"I need to check something out. Hold on."

Katie wandered closer. Trying not to be noticed, she peeked inside the glass window. Mesmerized by what she saw inside, she stood transfixed...watching.

"Katie, are you there? What's going on?"

"I—you are not going to believe what I'm seeing," Katie said, struggling to breathe. "Seriously."

Katie heard a baby cry. Christel groaned on the other end of the phone. "I got to go. What are you seeing?"

Katie went wide-eyed. "Oh, my goodness! Call Evan and have him take the kids. Get showered and call our brothers. We need a meeting!"

23

Katie perched nervously on the corner booth seat at Charley's, a place she and her siblings often headed for after Aiden and Shane's ballgames in Pā'ia. Despite the line at the door, she'd been seated right away. The owner was a friend of their family and a customer. Pali Maui delivered cases of fresh pineapples to them every morning.

She checked her watch for the third time when the door opened, and she spotted Christel, followed by Aiden and Shane.

Katie waved them over. "There you are. Took you long enough."

"Is it Mom?" Christel demanded, hair wet and looking like she'd just jumped out of the shower.

"Sort of."

Shane slid in beside Katie. "Spill. What's up?"

"Yeah, sounded urgent." Shane planted himself and grabbed the menu off the table.

Katie frowned. "Really, Shane? You always order the same thing."

"Ha, you're right." He flung the menu back to the table.

A waitress showed up with an order pad and pen. She directed her attention to Shane first. "Okay, buddy, what can I get for you?"

Katie exchanged looks across the table at Christel. Her older sister made a point of clearing her throat while Aiden tried to hide his amusement as he turned to the waitress. "Bro here, will have poached eggs and a stack of pancakes, hold the butter, and bring extra syrup." He looked at his brother. "Did I get it right?"

Without waiting for an answer, Aiden folded his menu and handed it to the waitress. "Biscuits and gravy, please. Two eggs. Over easy. And a side of bacon." He paused. "With pancakes."

Katie cleared her throat as if choking. "You sure that's enough?"

Aiden laughed her off. "What? I'm hungry."

Christel ordered an omelet. "Hold the hashbrowns."

"I'll eat 'em," Aiden offered.

Katie put in her order for a bowl of granola with fresh fruit topped with skim milk. She had to watch her weight.

Shane turned up his nose.

"What? You don't have to eat it." She drew a deep breath. "Okay, guys. I have to tell you something important."

They all gave her their attention. "Yeah, what's up?" Shane asked, reaching for a packet of sugar. "Why did we have to drop everything and rush over here?"

Katie drew a deep breath, preparing to reveal what she'd seen. "I saw Tom today. I was shopping and coming out the door of that cute new shop that opened at the Shops in Wailea. He was entering the store next door." She took a drink from her glass of water. "The store was a jewelry store."

Aiden let his back fall against the banquette. "So?"

Katie rolled her eyes. Her brothers could be so dense. "So, Tom went into a jewelry store. That alone begs the question as to why? So, I stayed out of sight and followed him. Well, not exactly trailed him inside. I peeked through the window."

Christel fingered the utensils on the table in front of her. "And?"

Katie leaned forward. "He sidled up to the glass case that held the rings...diamond rings. I watched as he examined several selections, and then he chose one!"

"You think it's for Mom?" Shane asked.

"Oh, my goodness. You can be so lame. Who do you think it was for?"

Christel's eyebrows lifted. "Uh, yeah. That's big. Do you think it was an engagement ring?"

The impact finally hit her brothers. They responded in unison, "Tom is going to ask Mom to marry him?"

Katie nodded, enjoying being the one in the know. "It certainly looks that way."

Aiden shook his head. "It's too soon for that."

Shane shoulder-bumped his brother. "C'mon, bro. It's been well over a year."

Christel frowned. "But Mom and Dad were married for nearly thirty-five years. She can't just move on too quickly. Rebound relationships are just that...rebounds. If Mom marries again, she needs to fully heal first before committing to someone else."

"Rebound has nothing to do with this," Katie argued. "I've watched them together. They're definitely in love."

"He treats her pretty good," Shane said. "I mean, if she's ready for that step, Tom is a good man."

Aiden shook his head a second time. "She's not ready."

His brother laughed. "Oh, this...coming from a guy who rarely dates."

Aiden lifted his chin. "I'm dating."

"Get out!" Shane had disbelief in his eyes. "The day you

commit to a woman is the same day I'll eat some of Katie's granola...even if it does taste like wood chips floating in milk."

"Granola is good for you," Katie protested. She turned to her oldest brother. "You're dating?"

"Who?" Shane demanded.

"Meghan McCord," Aiden announced, his face filled with a wide smile.

"That chick you work with?" Shane asked. "The one with the tiger tat down her arm? I mean, that's a lot of woman, right there."

"You're her manager," Christel reminded. "Do I need to jog your memory and tell you that your sister is a lawyer? You never date employees. The legal implications are—"

"Meghan doesn't work for me anymore."

"What happened?" Katie asked.

"She quit." Aiden's grin widened. "She took a job with a helicopter emergency service on O'ahu, but she'll be stationed here on Maui. We'll still work together fairly regularly. Most importantly, we'll spend a lot of time together after work hours." He winked.

"That's wonderful!" Katie exclaimed. She turned to Shane, a wide grin forming on her face. "Should I put in an order for extra granola? 'Cuz I'm not sharing mine."

As if on cue, the waitress returned to the table with their food.

Christel picked up her fork and dug into her breakfast as soon as her plate hit the table. "What?" she said when she noticed them all staring. "I'm starving. You try eating with two babies parked on your hips and see how much food you get in your mouth."

Katie took a bite of her granola. "Well, I'm happy for you, Aiden. It looks like love is blooming all around."

Shane suddenly choked.

"Are you okay?" Katie asked. "Aiden, hurry. Pat him on the back."

Shane waved off her concern. "I'm fine." He pointed in the direction of the entrance. "Looks like love really is in the air."

There stood their scruffy old uncle, Captain Jack, with his arm around the waist of a beautiful and very classy-looking woman...the lady from child protective services.

24

"Your brother is seeing someone?" Tom loaded the picnic basket into his trunk. "For real?"

Ava nodded and tucked a blanket in beside the basket. "For real. My kids called me from the restaurant to see if I knew. I didn't, of course. Jack doesn't shout his personal life from the rooftops."

"Well, good for him," Tom shut the trunk door and followed her to the passenger seat. When she was inside, he leaned in for a quick kiss before closing the door.

"Everyone acts so surprised," Ava said when Tom slipped in beside her. "The truth is Jack has always had a very healthy love life. Especially when he was younger."

"That's hard to imagine."

"Jack may not look like a heartthrob, but in high school, girls flocked to him in the hall. Even the popular ones. I remember this one—a sweet, blonde thing that looked like she stepped off the set of a sitcom—well, she moved to the island, and immediately every guy had his eyes set on dating her, especially the captain of the football team. Even the surfers followed after her. The boys trailed her like puppy dogs, trying to claim her attention."

Ava pulled her seat belt across her torso and fastened it. "Jack was not one of them. Perhaps that was the attraction. My brother was smart, but as I said, Jack wasn't going to grace magazine covers with his appearance." She laughed. "Back then, he dressed a lot like he does today—buttons missing, stains on his clothes, and mismatched prints. Much to the teachers' dismay, he started chewing on an unlit cigar in his junior year."

Tom started the engine. "Some people have it...that thing that draws people. It's unexplained. But I see it all the time."

Ava nodded. "Well, my brother has it...whatever *it* is." She leaned back against the plush leather seat. "I'm happy for him. No one should be alone in life."

When Tom didn't reply, she looked across the seat. "What?"

His smile filled with nervous tension. "Huh?"

"You have a look."

Tom shook his head. "No look."

"Yes, you do," Ava argued. "I've rarely seen you with that expression, but you definitely have it now."

His lips lifted slightly higher at the corners. "You're dreaming, Ava. There's no look." Then, changing the subject, "So, where are we going to picnic? I was thinking 'Ohe'o Gulch."

"The Seven Sacred Pools? But that's nearly two hours away."

"Which is why we're starting out so early. I'm in the mood for a beautiful setting, and the waterfalls are just the ticket. We could swim a bit after our picnic before heading home."

"I didn't pack a suit."

He grinned wolfishly.

Ava gave him a mock glare. "For the record, I don't skinny dip, especially with tourists nearby. Besides, it's rare that the pools are open for swimming after that big lawsuit a few years back."

He brushed off her concerns with a wave of his hand. "That's why this is the perfect place. I did some work for one of the park rangers. He assured me we could have access to some secluded areas." His grin widened. "It'll be only us."

Ava's brows lifted. "Wow. I had no idea I ran with someone with that kind of influence."

"So, what do you say? 'Ohe'o Gulch?"

"Okay. But I'm still not sure about the swimming part."

Tom laughed. "Okay, swimming is optional."

The Road to Hana had long been a favorite of Ava's. Hana didn't just hit you; it seeped into you. The entire area was like stepping back in time. Living on Maui, she had driven it many times. The peace of the quaint town of Hana could fully penetrate her soul.

In years past, she and Lincoln had taken the children often, stopping at the black sand beach and Ke'anae, sometimes with Elta, Alani, and their family. The kids all loved the milkshakes at The Preserve Kitchen and Bar. The little hole-in-the-wall eatery with wooden picnic tables inside was jokingly referred to as Hana's version of fine dining.

Now, the drive held not only good memories but some painful ones as well. On one of these sharp curves, Lincoln lost his life in a car accident returning from his tryst with Alani's adult daughter. Ava would never forget discovering Lincoln had secretly purchased a house in Hana where he spent time with Mia.

"What's the matter, Ava? You look sad."

She looked across at Tom. She had confided much of the story about Lincoln, but only some of the details. She wasn't up for doing it now. Her hand reached out, and she squeezed his arm. "Memories...good and bad."

He seemed to pick up on her nuanced response immediately. "Oh," was all he said. "Well, I intend to make good memories today. It's a promise." The nervous smile returned.

"There's that look again." She frowned with curiosity. "You're not acting yourself."

He shrugged. "You read far too much into things." Still, the look on his face portrayed a man with a secret. Her children often displayed the same look on Christmas morning when they could barely contain their anticipation for what was to come.

They reached their destination sooner than expected. Tourist traffic was light today, and Tom drove straight through to Hana, where they stopped to use the restroom, then continued on the few miles to the pools.

Tom pulled into a nearly empty parking area and cut the engine. "See? I told you we'd have the place to ourselves."

"There are tourists here," Ava argued as she exited the car.

"Not where we're going," he promised.

They unloaded Tom's SUV and carried the picnic supplies down a narrow winding path known as the Pīpīwai Trail.

Ava suddenly stopped.

"What is it?" Tom asked, slowing as he followed her.

She pointed. "Look!"

Tom gazed in the direction of where she pointed. "What am I looking at?"

Ava dropped the blanket and dug inside her bag. She pulled out a pair of binoculars and quickly brought them to her face, adjusting the lens. "A kolea, also known as a golden plover. Those little black-and-white-faced birds are a rare sight. They fly over twenty-five hundred miles every year to Alaska for the summer, returning to Hawai'i after mating." She pulled the binoculars from her face and offered them to Tom. "In all my years on the island, I've only seen them a couple of times."

Tom took the glasses and focused in. "Sure enough. There's two of them."

Ava nodded. "Yes, they always travel in pairs. Bird experts say they mate for life."

Tom smiled. "A love like that is worth following anywhere. Even on a long transcontinental flight."

Ava stared at her friend's face. There was that look again.

Behind them, they could hear tourists approaching. The birds took flight and landed on a distant taro leaf, nearly too far to see. Ava folded her glasses and placed them back into her bag. "Guess they wanted some privacy, too."

The volcanic dirt trail leading to the main pool wound through thick foliage with tall trees creating a canopy overhead. Thin streams of light broke through the leaves, creating a dappled pattern on the ground. Deep red dragon flowers and bright green leaves called elephant ears lined the Palikea Stream filled with mountain water that would eventually flow into the ocean.

"I'd forgotten how beautiful it is here," Ava remarked, looking all around.

"Stunning," Tom said with a swift glance at her before crossing a wooden footbridge.

A few minutes later, they entered a bamboo forest. The thin trunks filled with tiny green leaves reached to the sky, so thick the light on the trail dimmed.

The tourists' voices faded as Tom led her off the main trail and onto a lesser-used pathway through the bamboo. Several yards later, they entered an open area filled with lush grass surrounded by thick, jungle-like foliage. In the far distance, you could see the ocean, blue and sparkling in the sunlight.

Even though she'd lived on the island for nearly all her adult life, views like this never grew old.

"Are you getting tired?" Tom asked.

Ava shook her head. "No, but I can't help but stop and take a minute to appreciate the scenery."

He joined her and slipped his hand in hers. "How could

anyone see this stunning panorama and not believe in a Creator?"

"I agree."

Minutes later, they headed in the direction of another path.

"Where are you taking me?" Ava said, following him into the trees.

"You'll see." Tom grinned back at her. "I promise it's secluded."

Their destination was only a few minutes ahead. A rim of lava bordered a pool filled with blue water so clear Ava could see every stone on the shallow bottom. Further on, the pool deepened. Then she saw what he'd hinted at...a series of water-falls cascading several feet over a rock ledge.

"Do you like it?"

"Like it? I love it!" Unlike the pools with falls visited by most tourists, this waterfall was secluded and untouched—their own private playground.

"I thought you would. So that you know, we're no longer on the park property. This land is private and belongs to the man I referred to earlier. We're all alone."

He took the blanket from her hand and spread it on a flat surface overlooking the water. Then he opened the picnic basket and pulled out the food Ava had packed.

"Jon made us some ham sandwiches with pineapple relish."

Tom pulled his shirt over his head and used it to dab his damp forehead before tossing it onto the blanket. The temps were growing warmer as the morning turned to afternoon. Their hike had made it feel even hotter.

Ava stared at his bare chest and swallowed. "Jon said...uh, the relish has a touch of heat."

Tom unwrapped the sandwich Ava handed him. He smiled at her before taking a bite.

Ava watched him silently chew, finding it hard to breathe. She was a grandmother, but she could still appreciate a muscled chest.

As if reading her thoughts, Tom grinned. "You know, we could swim in our underwear if skinny dipping is beyond your comfort level. That would be nearly the same as wearing swimsuits."

Ava slowly unwrapped her sandwich. "Yeah, that might work." She'd had no inclination to go swimming today, but several factors were making her reconsider that decision. Tom's chest, and the inviting water in that pool.

When they'd finished their lunch, Ava lifted her chin. "Okay, let's go."

"Swimming?"

"Yes, you're right. Our underwear can serve as our swimsuits." She could justify that in her mind, even with Alani's firm religious beliefs echoing in her mind.

They quickly cleaned up their lunch remains, and then they stripped down. Ava carefully folded their discarded garments and laid them next to the picnic basket. "Any idea on what we'll use for towels?" She avoided checking out the barely clothed man beside her.

"We'll cross that when we come to it," he told her, his eyes boldly lingering on her. "At the very least, we can take turns drying off with the picnic blanket."

Like kids, they scrambled to the water, hand in hand, and jumped in.

The water was cool and refreshing, not cold. Even so, a shiver of excitement brought goosebumps to Ava's skin. It felt good to shed all the expectations and demands of her life and instead focus on having fun. Focus on Tom.

He took her hand and brought it to his lips. "Do you know how beautiful you are?"

Ava swam into his embrace, enjoying the feel of his skin

against her own. They lingered several minutes before she finally pulled back and splashed him with water, like a teenager. Then, together, they swam toward the cascading waterfall. Droplets sprayed over them as the water plunged into the pool below.

She pulled her hair up in her hands and wrung the strands while treading water in place.

Tom pointed. "Look, Ava! The sunlight shining through the mist is creating a rainbow."

The arc of colors nearly brought tears to her eyes. Rainbows were a sign of hope, the beauty after the storm, representing good fortune and promise.

The past couple of years had been riddled with twists, turns, and unexpected surprises. Ava and her family had faced so many difficult things—the loss of a husband and father, Aiden in the boat explosion, and the storm that threatened Pali Maui and everything they held dear. Most recently, Christel had struggled with infertility. It had been a lot to deal with.

The rainbow was like the heavens winking, telling her that good things lay ahead.

Floating, they drifted to the edge of the pool. Tom climbed out first, then held out a hand to Ava, helping her from the water.

The only thought running through her head at that moment was how much she enjoyed this man. He had filled an empty place, and she was grateful for his friendship.

He scurried for the blanket, gathered it up, and brought it around her shoulders, tucking himself in beside her.

"Ava, I have something important I want to say to you."

She looked at him and saw that expression again. "What is it? Is something wrong?"

"Let's get dressed."

She nodded and pulled on her clothes, not caring that her

underwear underneath was still damp. Tom did the same. It would dry quickly.

He took her hand. "You know, I've been doing a lot of thinking lately."

"You have?"

A rumble in the distance pulled their attention. Ava was surprised to see dark skies looming in the distance. "Tom, I think it's going to rain."

Hana was a beautiful place, green and lush. The rainforest mecca could turn ugly quickly when it stormed. The steep mountainsides were known for sudden downpours.

Seven Sacred Pools often got up to twenty days of rain every month, even in the island's dry season. Many of the storms could turn violent in a matter of minutes, creating flash floods and downslope winds clocking in at over eighty miles per hour.

Clearly disappointed, Tom grabbed her hand. "We need to pack up and get out of here."

Taking his lead, Ava scrambled to gather their things. Together, they ran for the car and tossed everything in the back. Before they could climb inside the vehicle, the sky opened and drenched the area with rain.

Ava closed the door, already soaked.

She looked across at Tom, who was also dripping wet. "Well, that didn't end well."

An unusually cross look passed over his features. "No...the day sure didn't go as planned."

25

_____

By the time Tom and Ava pulled into the yard at Pali Maui, the sun was out and shining brightly. Despite her prodding, Tom wouldn't tell her what had been on his mind before the storm broke. In fact, he seemed a little distracted on the drive home.

"Tom, before we go inside, I have to ask—did I do or say something that hurt you, or—"

Tom quickly assured her that was not the case. "I was only disappointed that our fun day was cut short, that's all."

She patted his hand. "Regardless of the storm, I had an absolutely lovely time, Tom. I hope we can do it again very soon." She leaned in and kissed his cheek.

"Hey, Mom!"

Ava turned to see both of her girls heading their way. Each had a baby in their arms. Little Noelle straggled behind Katie, her thumb in her mouth.

Ava climbed from the car. "Hi, girls. What's up?"

They exchanged amused glances. "We were going to ask you the same," Katie said with a wide grin.

Confused, Ava moved to the back of the SUV to help Tom retrieve her things. "It was a lovely day."

"And..." Christel prodded.

Ava frowned. "Is something up with you two? Why the questions?"

Tom pulled the blanket and picnic basket out of his vehicle, and Ava followed him inside. "You girls hungry?"

Katie shrugged her shoulders. "No, we're good. You two good?"

Ava's frown deepened. "Come again?"

Her girls exchanged another look before Christel responded, "Everything's fine."

They smiled weakly at Tom. "Well, I've got to get home," Katie said with a puzzled expression.

Christel nodded. "Me, too, I guess."

Ava gave them each a hug before following Tom inside.

"What do you think is up with those two?" She took the blanket from his hands and headed for the laundry room. "They were acting strange," she hollered over her shoulder.

She placed the blanket into the washing machine, tossed in some soap, and turned the appliance on. Then she joined Tom back in the living room.

"Do you want a glass of wine?" she offered.

His hands plunged inside his pants pocket. "Nah, I think I'll pass." He moved to join her and pulled her into a kiss. His lips lingered. When he finally pulled away, he looked her directly in the eyes. "Listen, you think you could get away again tomorrow?"

She hesitated. "Oh, I don't know. As much as I'd like to, with Christel gone on maternity leave, there's a lot on my plate here at Pali Maui. I'm not sure I can play hooky two days in a row."

She saw his disappointment. "How about tomorrow evening? We could do something tomorrow night after work hours."

His face brightened as he considered her offer. "Sure, that'll work. It's a date." He paused. "Tell you what, why don't you come to my house, and I'll fix you something special for dinner."

Ava nodded. "Sounds wonderful. What are we having?"

"It's a surprise."

There was that look again.

～

AVA STOOD at Tom's door wearing a pretty sleeveless dress in a shade of apricot. Her mother's strand of pearls adorned her neck.

While waiting for Tom to answer, she fingered the pearls. Her daughters both thought they were a bit stuffy. "What are you, Mom? A Barbara Bush wannabe?" Katie had asked her.

Christel laughed at her sister's comment. "You know why oysters don't share their pearls?" She paused. "Because they're *shellfish*."

Ava ignored them and insisted on wearing the memento despite her girls' bad jokes.

The door opened. "There you are." Tom wiped his hands on a dish towel and leaned in to kiss her cheek. "Come on in."

"Oh, my goodness. Something smells delicious."

He motioned for her to follow him into the kitchen. "I put a prime rib beef roast in the oven. And baked potatoes." He checked his watch. "Dinner should be ready within a half hour." He winked. "By the way, with the help of your son-in-law, I got my hands on one of those Japanese Wagyu roasts. He promises that the extra fat and marbling will enhance the flavor."

"Jon's the expert."

"I think I have it all under control." Tom tossed the towel on the marble countertop. "Let's have a pre-dinner cocktail on the lanai."

Even though they'd been dating for months, Ava had only been at Tom's house less than a half dozen times. His place reflected him perfectly—with stone walls and rich leather furnishings. He used a mix of classic pieces with earth tones and modern items in chrome. The main wall was adorned with a collection of framed golf photos. There was one of Tom and Tiger Woods and another image of him standing in a line of men with the famous Hogan footbridge on the Augusta National golf course in the background.

She paused on the way out to the lanai for a better look. "Oh, my goodness! Tom! Is that Arnold Palmer?"

He nodded. "Yeah, he was good friends with my dad. Arnie was instrumental in helping me get my start in this business, much to my parents' chagrin. As you learned in Boston, they had other plans for my career path."

Yes, she had. After a trip to his family's home and a face-to-face meeting with his mother, a lot became clear. Thankfully, Tom was his own man and didn't fold to the whims of others. He lovingly set Frances Strobe straight before returning to Maui with Ava.

He'd put her first, and that felt good.

On the lanai, Tom fixed her an old-fashioned, plopping a deep red cherry in the center of the glass next to a thin slice of orange peel. The bourbon cocktail was his favorite drink.

"Thank you." She took the glass and surveyed his yard. The pool was impeccable, built in what looked like a grotto. While not as stunning as the falls they'd seen yesterday, the ambiance was a close second.

She noticed a single red rose on the table.

"For you," he told her.

Touched by the gesture, she picked it up and brought the fragrant bloom to her nose. "Thank you, Tom. It's lovely."

Tom took a sip of this cocktail, sat next to her on the patio sofa, and reached for her hand. "Ava, I hope you know how special you are to me," he began. "I love you in the way a puppy loves—devoted, playful, trusting. I suppose I should be ashamed of that somehow. Aren't men supposed to be tough?"

Ava's insides fluttered. "What are you saying, Tom?"

"I'm saying I am strong—strong enough to risk being broken all over again. I've known the heartbreak of divorce and the heartache of lost hopes and dreams when it comes to love. Ava, you are worth risking it all again. I guess what I'm trying to say is that all I have left of my heart is yours."

Ava looked back at him and squeezed his hand. "Oh, Tom. I feel the same."

Suddenly, a loud alarm sounded.

Tom frantically glanced around. "What the hell is that?"

He leaped from the sofa and rushed inside the house. Ava followed.

Inside, thick smoke billowed from the kitchen, specifically from the oven.

"Oh no!" Tom shouted. "Ava, get back!"

She did as she was instructed. "Do you want me to call 911?"

"No need. The alarm is wired to alert emergency services automatically."

Tom coughed as he yanked open a drawer and pulled out a fire extinguisher.

"Oh, Tom. Be careful," Ava warned. She waved the smoke away from her face.

He stepped carefully to the double oven and opened the bottom door. Smoke and heat pushed him back. "No flames," he yelled. "Call Aiden and tell him not to come. I got this."

Ava hesitated.

"Call him," Tom repeated. He pulled the pin on the extinguisher and blasted a white cloud at the oven.

She went for her phone and pushed the stored number for

her son. "What's up, Mom? Oh, we've got a call coming in. I've got to go."

"Wait!" she yelled into the phone. "It's Tom's house. An automatic alarm. There's no fire, and he thinks he's got everything under control."

Aiden paused. His muffled shouts alerted his team that it was a false alert, and the alarm in the station ceased to sound. "Okay, Mom. Are you sure everything's okay?"

"Yes, there's smoke damage, but no fire. Sorry for the bother."

"Well, okay." Aiden paused. "So, you're over at Tom's?" The tone in his voice changed.

"I told you I was."

"Okay, well...that's great. I mean, really great."

"Aiden, what's the matter with you?"

"Nothing. Just...well, have a good time, Mom."

Ava shook her head. Why was her son acting so odd? Especially on the tail of a near-miss fire? She bid him goodbye and hung up, then returned to the kitchen. "Okay, fire trucks called off."

All the windows were open, and Tom used the kitchen towel to wave the smoke outside. Thankfully, the room looked a little better, despite the acrid smell.

"Boy, Tom. I'm afraid you'll have to get a special cleaning service to remove the smoke residue from your walls." She swiped her finger across the paint, leaving a noticeable streak.

Tom rubbed the back of his neck. "Well, strike two. Another date down the drain." He got that look again.

"Oh, honey...everything was lovely. Well, until—"

Tom sighed. "Yeah, until. We could try again this weekend?" He looked like he wanted to say more but fell into a coughing fit.

"I think we'd best get out of here until the smoke completely clears," Ava warned.

On the way home, Ava's phone rang. It was Christel. "So, Aiden called."

Ava confirmed the events of the evening. "It was awful. Tom went to all this effort to cook for me. The fat in the beef overheated and created smoke. He's going to have to have his kitchen walls professionally cleaned."

"I'm so sorry, Mom. But—" Her daughter paused. "Is that all that happened tonight?"

Ava frowned. What in the world was up with her kids? They were all acting so strange. "Wasn't alarms and smoke enough adventure?"

"Are you seeing Tom again soon?"

"Not that it's any of your business, Miss Snoopy, but yes. We plan to go out again this weekend."

She could audibly hear her daughter sigh. "Oh, good. That's good."

26

After a full day out in the fields with Mig, Ava was filled with anticipation as she dressed for her date with Tom. He was taking her dancing.

She found herself humming as she pulled three dresses from the back of her closet and placed them on the bed. Goodness, how long had it been since she wore any of these? Would they still fit?

The first was a simple black sheath—elegant, but far too plain. Reminded her too much of the one she wore to Lincoln's funeral, which she burned after learning of Mia.

She put the dress back and picked up the next one. She loved the silky rose-colored fabric, but the length was too long for dancing.

Ah, this one. She lifted the last dress and knew she'd found the right one. The ice-blue knee-length little number was cut in a straight line with a sheer overlay decorated with tiny silver flowers.

She held it up to her and gazed in the floor-length mirror. Perfect!

Besides that, she had a pair of shoes that complemented the

dress—a pair of glittery silver Christian Louboutin stilettos with sleek, elegant lines. The heels were nearly four inches. Could she pull that off?

Ava looked back into the mirror. Of course, she could. She wasn't yet fifty-five.

She grinned and pulled the shoe box off the top of her closet.

After taking a long hot bubble bath, she toweled off and put on her makeup, taking special care to outline her lips before applying a glossy shade of peach. Subtle but perfect with the dress color.

She wrapped her hair into an elegant chignon and fastened it securely in place. Next, she put on a pair of diamond studs. She didn't need anything more in terms of jewelry. The dress carried the look.

She spritzed her favorite cologne, a sumptuous blend of freesia and orange flower. It was one of Tom's favorites, as well.

Ava wanted this evening to be perfect. Goodness knows, the last two occasions where she'd spent time with Tom had ended badly. Not that either of them needed an occasion to enjoy each other's company. Simply being with him was enough for her. He likely felt the same.

Still, she was looking forward to the special evening ahead. Tom had reservations at a newly opened dinner club called Kealoha, the Hawaiian word for love. The place had been billed as the perfect romantic setting. The evening would include dinner overlooking the ocean and dancing under the stars.

Tom picked her up promptly at seven. "Oh, my goodness. Ava, you look stunning." He stepped back for another look, then pulled her into his arms. "I'm the luckiest man alive."

She couldn't help but smile. "I'm not sure about that, and you don't look half bad yourself." He was dressed in tan-colored slacks with a suit jacket, no tie. His loafers were casual yet made of fine leather.

"Okay, you ready?" he asked.

"Yes, let me grab my wrap." Maui rarely got cold this time of the year, but the evenings could bring a light breeze.

When they arrived at Kealoha, the maître d quickly seated them at a table overlooking the ocean's edge. Tiki torches surrounded the dining area, their flames blazing against a night sky filled with stars.

"This is lovely," she murmured as Tom held out the chair for her. The night smelled like plumeria, salt mist, and fresh grass.

The simple menu offered a choice of two pre-selected entrées with several additional courses, both before and after their main meal. They chose the same entrée, a wonderful grilled steak—in honor of the beef they hadn't gotten to eat the other night.

Despite being stuffed, they both ordered the featured dessert item—a seven-layer coconut cake with alternating banana and mango filling. A mound of freshly made whipped crème topped the thing. "How in the world do you eat this?" Ava asked, with her fork poised to find out.

She slid a bite inside her mouth and closed her eyes for a moment, savoring the tropical flavors.

Tom smiled, reached across the small tabletop, and wiped whipped cream from her mouth using his forefinger, startling her. He popped his finger in his own mouth. "Mmm..."

He stared at her with an intense gaze that made her uncomfortable yet warmed her heart at the same time. The corners of her mouth lifted in a timid smile. "What?"

"Do you know how beautiful you are?" He cocked his head to the side, and his eyes filled with emotion. "You are an amazing woman, Ava. Every day, I admire how you take on your world, always with a smile on your face. Nothing detracts from your determination to feel joy. I know life handed you some tough stuff. You've weathered it all with dignity and grace."

His praise was appreciated, if not a little embarrassing. "Every flower has to grow through dirt," she said in an attempt to lighten the moment.

Tom nodded. "True. But, I want you to know how much I admire you." He paused. "And, how much you mean to me."

Two string musicians joined a cellist on the raised podium. A hush fell over the tables as they tuned their instruments, then began playing the first strains of a song Ava loved—"Unchained Melody."

Tom stood and held out his hand. "May I have this dance?"

"I'd love that." Ava wiped the corners of her mouth with the linen napkin and placed it on the table. She stood, and Tom led her to the area designated for dancing. Strings of lights beamed overhead.

Ava rested her head against Tom's shoulder as he placed his hand on her back and they slowly began swaying to the music. She could feel the heat of his skin and hear his heartbeat. He smelled of bergamot and musk, a rugged yet fresh scent she found intoxicating. It was a heady moment she never wanted to end.

The music wound to a close. Tom leaned close and whispered in her ear, "Let's get out of here. I have something important I want to ask you." His voice was husky and filled with longing.

Back at the table, he waved over their waiter and quickly closed out the bill. Then, he led her down the steps leading to a boardwalk extending over a craggy rock shelf. Gentle waves created a lullaby as the water slapped against the pillars. The wind whispered through the palms behind them.

Ava dutifully walked alongside him, no longer able to contain her curiosity. "What do you want to ask me, Tom?"

He stopped and turned. The heat from his eyes warmed her

all over as his hand went to his pocket, drawing out a small black velvet box.

Ava's eyes immediately widened, and she found herself unable to breathe. Was he...was that a ring?

She stepped forward to take his face in her hands, needing to touch the crest of his cheek, and traced the edges of his jawline to the cleft of his chin.

She felt a stirring for more. Much more.

This was it. This was why he'd had all those strange looks. He was going to ask her to marry him.

"Oh, Tom."

Suddenly, her heel caught in a slivered opening in the wood, toppling her sideways. She involuntarily yelped and tried to right herself. The motion only served to overcorrect, and she listed to the left.

Tom tried to catch her to no avail.

The heel broke and she went down...hard. "Ouch!" she yelled. "My ankle!"

Tom crouched to her side. "Oh, my goodness! Ava, are you all right?"

She couldn't hold back the tears. "I think I sprained my ankle."

He lifted her into a sitting position and raised the offending ankle to get a better look. "Oh no. I think you're right. It's swelling."

Without another word, he scooped her into his arms, leaving her broken shoe behind. Trying to ignore the pain, Ava wrapped her arms around his neck and leaned her head against his chest.

Her ankle throbbed as he carried her back to the restaurant.

27

"Well, what do we have here?" Evan moved into the hospital room, wearing a white coat with a stethoscope draped around his neck. He carried a digital clipboard.

"Mom was dancing and hurt her ankle," Christel told her husband. "Looks like a sprain."

"I was not dancing," Ava protested. "I was on a wooden pier. My heel caught in the opening between the slats, and I went down." Her remaining Christian Louboutin heel was perched on the hospital table beside the ER bed.

Evan lifted the white coverlet and examined his mother-in-law's ankle. "Ouch! Looks painful," he said as he pressed lightly around the black and blue flesh. When Ava grimaced, he replaced the blanket over her legs. "Let's get an X-ray. That'll give us the information we need to rule out a break. But I agree. Looks like a sprain. If you're really unlucky, perhaps a torn ligament."

Ava groaned. Another night ruined, and what looked to be weeks ahead on crutches.

"But she's going to be okay?" Tom asked, his face filled with concern.

Evan nodded and turned his attention back to Ava. "Do you hurt anywhere else? Your back?"

She shook her head. "No. Just the ankle." She turned to Tom. "I'm so sorry."

"Ava, quit apologizing. It was an accident. I'm sorry I had you out there while you were wearing those shoes. I should have known it was dangerous."

A commotion outside the door drew their attention. Katie barged into the room, followed by Aiden and Shane. Captain Jack was close behind.

"What's the deal?" Katie asked, her voice trembling.

"Mom's fine," Christel told her. "Likely just a bad sprain."

Katie sighed with relief. Her eyes immediately went to Ava's left hand. "Then, everything was interrupted...again?"

Tom cleared his throat. "Look, I don't know how you girls seem to know, but it's time I clear this up." He turned to Ava and took her hand. "For days, I've been attempting to tell you what's on my heart. Each time my special plans were thwarted. First, the storm drove us away from the romantic waterfall. A burned roast ruined my attempt to pull this off poolside. Then, your fall interrupted my scheme tonight. I'd hoped to create something special, something memorable...like in the movies." He ran his hands through the top of his hair. "I give up."

After pulling his suit jacket off and laying it over the end of the hospital bed, Tom dug into his pocket and pulled out the little velvet box. He sat on the bed beside Ava and took her hand.

He looked around the room at everyone standing. "It's time to make the memory—right here. Right now."

"Oh, my goodness!" Katie clasped her hands together.

Aiden and Shane's faces broke into wide smiles.

Even Evan couldn't help but grin. "Well, go for it," he urged, laying his clipboard on the hospital table.

Not needing any further encouragement, Tom cleared his throat. "Ava, I'm so grateful for you. I'm grateful that we met. I'm grateful that somehow in this crazy universe with infinite possibilities, destiny paved the way so we could see each other at the right time, at the right place, in the right moment. So many things could have happened to keep us from existing together. Yet we met and started something so beautiful."

His eyes filled with emotion. "Sweetheart, I never thought I'd marry again, but you've changed the rhythm of my heart. The love I never knew I needed, I found in you." He brought her hand to his mouth and kissed her palm. "From this moment onwards, I don't want to walk alone. I want to walk with you. I want to fight for you when you give up, make you smile when it's hard to find happiness, and be your safe place when you need comfort. You're mine, and I'm crazy in love with you. I can't imagine my life without you."

Tom opened the box, removed a stunning diamond ring—a three-carat solitaire set on a brilliant gold band—and offered it to Ava. "Will you marry me?"

Ava's heart nearly thumped out of her chest. Never had she planned on this friendship becoming more necessary to her than the air she breathed. She'd learned relationships were risky. Committing her heart to someone else forever was a decision she knew not to take lightly.

There was no choice, really. Any future felt bleak without him by her side. She swallowed and glanced around at her beaming children before turning her full attention back to Tom. "Oh, Tom. Yes! I'll marry you."

28

J ack got out of his beat-up Chevy and sauntered into the Dirty Monkey, chewing on an unlit cigar. Inside, he scanned the dim room until his eyes found what he was looking for. He waved and headed in that direction.

"Hey, Maggie. Sorry I had to leave so abruptly last night. Or that I didn't call you. It was late when I got home from the hospital."

"No problem," she said, picking up her glass of wine. "Is your sister okay?"

"Yes. As the story has it, Tom took Ava for a romantic date at Kealoha intending to pop the question. He was about to bend to one knee and propose when she fell out on the boardwalk."

"Oh no! What a horrible thing to happen at such an important moment."

He slid into an empty seat at her table. "Yeah, sure cooked his goose on that one. Ava sprained her ankle." He let out a chuckle. "If you'd have seen the shoes she was wearing, you'd understand how it happened. The heels must've been this high," he motioned, exaggerating slightly. "All sparkly and with red soles underneath."

"Christian Louboutins," Maggie interjected.

"Huh?"

"Those shoes you described. They are Christian Louboutins. Very expensive."

He nodded and stroked his graying beard. "Ah, yeah. That figures."

"So, she ended up in the ER?"

Mole, the bartender, brought Jack a glass of his favorite whiskey. "So, how's the sister?"

As Jack repeated the story, his friend, Smitty Truant, picked up his drink from off the bar and joined them.

"Ah, bad break," he said.

Maggie leaned forward. "So, tell us. Did he ask your sister to marry him? I mean, after all that, did he still propose?"

"He sure did," Jack bellowed with loud laughter. "Right there in the ER. Not as romantic as he'd hoped, but the moment was special. The wedding is going to be amazing. And, you're all invited!"

Mole flipped a bar towel onto his shoulder. "Excellent news. And a good reason to celebrate. A round of drinks for every-one...on the house."

Jack turned his attention to Maggie, who sat looking as beautiful as ever. He went to bed every night wondering what an amazing gal like that had ever seen in the likes of him. He wasn't one to look a gift horse in the mouth. His plan was simply to ride out this good fortune for as long as she'd have him...or at least until she wised up and decided to move on to someone else. Truth be known. He prayed that wasn't for a good long time.

"Jack?" she asked, lifting her wine glass. She took a sip and peered at him over the rim of the goblet.

"Yeah, honey bunches."

"Do you think your nephew will have a date to the wedding?"

"Aiden? He's in a relationship. Some gal he met at work."

"No, the other one. The one with the little son."

"Oh, Shane. Yeah, he works for me."

"Does he have a date to the wedding?" she repeated. "Because I have a niece I think would be perfect for him."

29

The morning of the wedding dawned with the first signs of sunlight casting shades of mango and hues of lavender across the ocean. Ava stood and took the scene in, letting the beauty fill her up.

The past weeks had been a blur as Ava juggled the demands of Pali Maui with wedding preparations. Luckily, the sprain had not been as bad as earlier thought and healed quickly. The last thing she needed was to walk down the aisle with crutches.

She wanted a simple ceremony. Her girls and Alani had much more in mind. All of them had been very vocal about the need to make this day special.

"Let's hold the ceremony at the Wailea Chapel," Alani suggested. "We can line the aisle with swags of red roses and white hibiscus. After Elta pronounces you man and wife, we can release doves out the open windows."

"Oh, Alani. I think that's a bit over the top. This is a second marriage for both Tom and me. Neither of us want a lot of fuss."

Her girls had their own ideas. "The ceremony should be at

the crest of Haleakalā at sunrise, Mom. Just think of the metaphor with the sun rising from the cloud cover below."

Christel shook her head. "Do you really expect all the guests to get up in the middle of the night and trek up that winding road and stand out in the cold while Mom and Tom exchange their vows? That's simply not practical."

Even Willa had an opinion. "Grammy Ava, I think you and Tom should hold your wedding on a boat at night with white lights strung over top of the railings and violins playing in the background. How romantic!"

Ava laughed to herself. Yes, all of that sounded romantic. In the end, she'd remained firm. The ceremony would be on the beach, her special place, the setting that filled her soul. Her circle of friends and family would be there to witness their vows, but she stayed adamant that she wanted an intimate and meaningful day, not a production.

Ava climbed from her car, carrying a single envelope. She walked with purpose over to an opening in the rock wall and onto a beautiful pocket of sand lined with palms and plumeria trees with amazing views of Kahoʻolawe and Molokini. This spot was hidden and known to locals as Secret Cove.

It was where Lincoln proposed to her all those years ago.

Ava stood there basking in the beauty for several seconds before taking a deep breath, knowing she had unfinished business she had to attend to before moving on.

She opened the envelope and pulled out a letter she'd penned hours earlier while darkness still hovered over the island.

Dear Lincoln,

I survived. I survived the hurt and the pain, and so did our children. What you did...well, your actions were unspeakable. Yet, I found a way to forgive you and feel joy.

So did they.

Christel is now a mom of two darling twin babies. She remarried an amazing man, a doctor. Evan adores her.

Despite a few setbacks, like losing everything in a house fire, Katie continues to be enthusiastic and adventurous, taking on new projects with passion. Nothing seems to thwart her zest for life. Thankfully, I think Willa and Noelle are both going to take after their mom. I already see signs that they will become formidable women who will wring every ounce of happiness from their days on earth.

Aiden was promoted to captain down at the station. He continues to take life seriously, but recently, he did something completely out of character. He fell head-over-heels in love with a gal who is his exact opposite. She even has a tiger tattoo! He's the happiest I've ever seen him.

I know you worried that Shane was irresponsible. You couldn't have been more wrong on that. I wish you could see how he's pivoted from his wild lifestyle in order to be the kind of dad his little Carson needed. He adores his son. I'm so very proud of him...and I know you would be, too.

Yes, your family not only survived...but flourished. I am so very grateful.

Now, I look back on my time with you without the ache. I can remember the good and all the love we felt for one another. I did love you, Lincoln. And, while you foolishly chose darkness, I know you loved me, too. And our children.

Later today, I'm going to be a wife again.

Today marks a new day. I'll now be Ava Strobe.

I begin a new chapter with a new man, a new name, and a new life. This time, I confess I am terrified to love that hard again. Losing you changed me. Courage isn't my fearless go-to anymore. It's the default, the only choice left.

Tom is a good man. A man who loves me and will be faithful.

I intend to live well, Lincoln. Living well is a courageous thing to do. So, I have loved again, now fully knowing what it means to have all my chips on the table. It means I can lose. But it also means I can win. Big.

So, this is goodbye, Lincoln. Wherever you are...be well.

~Ava

She was surprised that no tears formed. Instead, something lifted. She felt lighter as she walked to the water's edge. Ava bent, placed the single sheet of paper upon an incoming wave, and stood, watching as the white foam took her message.

Then she turned...and walked away.

30

"Where in the world have you been?" Alani demanded as Ava entered the back door of the church.

Ava drew her best friend into a shoulder hug. "I had to close a door before walking into my new life."

She surveyed the scene where her daughters and Mia were putting the finishing touches on the wedding site and smiled. "Everything looks wonderful, Alani."

Her friend brightened. "We've worked hard to make everything perfect."

Ava sighed. "Ah, and it is."

A little compromise never hurt, especially when it came to making her loved ones happy.

Ava and Tom would indeed marry on a beach...the sandy stretch located at the edge of the church lawn. Strings of lights hung from the palms, and a trio of string musicians was poised to play. Swags of simple greenery hung from a white arch decorated with a few red roses and white hibiscus. While the ceremony would not be at the crest of Haleakalā, she and Tom would say their vows, silhouetted by the moon.

"Hurry," Alani urged. "The ceremony starts in less than an hour."

~

Ava took a final look in the mirror, satisfied with her reflection. She wore a simple white off-the-shoulder holoku without a train. Her hair was pulled up with curls cascading to her neck, with a single white plumeria tucked behind her ear.

"So, this is it," she murmured.

Alani pulled her into a light hug. "Yes, it's time." She gave her a quick peck on the cheek. "Remember, God's got this." She winked and then she was gone.

Ava waited a few moments, then followed. Her boys stood just outside the door. They extended their elbows, ready to walk her down the tiki-lined aisle.

She grinned and slipped her arms into theirs and looked out over the small crowd that had gathered.

There was Christel and Evan. A stroller with sleeping babies was parked near where they sat. Katie and Jon and their girls were next to them near the front. Mig and Wimberly Ann sat in the second row. Alani slipped in beside them. She patted Ori and Mia on the knees and turned to look at Ava.

Jack and his new lady friend, Maggie Williams, were seated one row over. A young blonde girl, her niece, turned and wiggled her fingers back at Shane. Shane beamed and waved back.

Halia and her daughter, Kina, were there. So was Ava's sister, Vanessa and her daughter, Isabelle.

These were the people who meant the most to her. They were gathered to share her special day.

Even Tom's mother had flown in from Boston for the event. Even more, she'd been extremely pleasant and gracious.

The violinists started playing, and the first strains of Pachelbel's "Canon in D" rang out, accompanied by the sound of the ocean waves.

"Ready, Mom?" Aiden asked.

She squeezed her boys' arms. "Ready."

At the end of the aisle, Tom waited next to Elta under the arch. Her fiancé wore a loose-fitting white shirt over casual slacks. A white floral lei hung around his neck. Her beloved man smiled at her with anticipation.

Ava's insides went giddy as she stepped forward and made her way to him.

Her boys lightly kissed the sides of her cheeks before they took their places next to their sisters.

Tom leaned toward her. "Do you hear that? My heart is pounding."

She whispered back, "Mine is pounding, too, just so you know."

He took her hand and squeezed, then nodded to Elta, signaling they were ready.

Elta straightened and cleared his throat.

"Dearly beloved who are gathered, we are so delighted each of you is here to witness the marriage of Tom Strobe and Ava Briscoe—a couple who have shown that second chances really do exist, that rainbows can sprout from ashes." He smiled at them. "It is my understanding that Tom and Ava would like to recite a few words before they complete their vows."

Tom took her hands in his, and looked at her with those deep blue eyes. He cleared his throat.

"Ava, today I promise you this: I will choose you every day, giving you the best I have and all of my faithfulness. I will love you with my words and my actions, my decisions, and my commitments. Every day of our life together, I will kiss you and make you laugh. I will remind you how beautiful you are to me. I will encourage you, I will listen to you, I will tell you what's on my heart. I will never give up our greatest advantage—knowing that God is the author of our love. I will honor Him by loving you with all that I have and all that I am, and I vow to make your life better than it was without me. You are my heart's song, the colors in my rainbow, and I will love you for as long as we both shall live."

Her lashes spiked with moisture, spilling over with happy tears. Ava swallowed, and she squeezed Tom's hand, barely able to push the words she'd memorized from her tight throat.

"Tom Strobe, I wasn't expecting you. In my wildest dreams, I had no idea we'd end up together. The single most extraordinary thing I've ever done with my life is falling in love with you. I've never been seen so completely—loved so passionately—protected so fiercely. In your eyes, I see my home. I see eternity. No matter what may come our way, I promise to always follow you, no matter where that might lead. I will honor you with my life and cherish you until I take my last breath. You are the colors in my rainbow—my heart's song. I love you."

They completed their vows, and Elta's face broke into a pleased grin. "And now, it is my extreme pleasure to pronounce you husband and wife. Tom, you may kiss your bride."

Tom obliged and pressed a tender kiss onto her lips.

The traditional Hawaiian conch shell blew, signaling marital hope and longevity.

Applause erupted from the small crowd. Her brother, Jack, pulled the unlit cigar from his mouth and yelled, "That's how it's done!"

Katie joined him and shouted, "Way to go, Mom!"

Ava couldn't help but weep with joy. A rainbow had indeed sprouted from the ashes.

She was Mrs. Tom Strobe—a woman wholly surrendered to a man who loved her—a man she could trust with her entire heart.

EPILOGUE

Hey, folks...Captain Jack here. Never mind me as I swipe this tear from my ruddy cheek. After reading these books, you know how much I love my sister. Now that was some wedding, huh? I get a little choked up just thinking about Ava's lifetime of happiness with Tom.

Of course, I have a new lady on my arm as well. Maggie may not look like someone who'd go for the likes of me, but 'ole Jack has his ways with women. *winks*

Ava and I aren't the only ones who found love in this story. My nephews finally caved in that department. Meghan will keep Aiden warm on lonely nights while Shane is getting to know Maggie's niece. I see good things ahead for both of those boys.

Ah, yes....love is in the air on Maui.

Hey, that's not all. I have a big surprise for you. *drumroll* The author of the Maui Series is with me today!"

Kellie waves. "Hi, everyone!"

So, is it true? Songs of the Rainbow is the last book in the Maui Series? That news is going to make a lot of folks pretty darn unhappy, including 'ole Captain Jack.

"Sadly, the answer is true—at least in part. All good things must come to an end eventually, and the adage is true of book series. The good news is that there will be a future holiday book HIBISCUS CHRISTMAS, so we'll all get to revisit the Briscoe family. As you know...I write for my readers. If I get a deluge of emails asking for more books set on Maui, I am here to serve. Especially if it requires another research trip to this tropical paradise!"

Kellie smiles. "Until then, a new series is in the development stages. I'm not ready to disclose the details, but the characters and setting have already deeply captured my heart. I think all of you will feel the same. Hint: there may be some mountains."

Jack chews on his unlit cigar. "Now that's worth celebrating with a drink of hooch! Great news! How can we stay in touch and learn more about this series and when the books will be available for preorder?"

"I highly recommend signing up for my newsletter. The retailers won't let me place links here in this epilogue. If you keep scrolling, I've provided links to all my books and my website."

Jack strokes his beard...Well, everyone! You heard it here first...a new series is on the horizon. Until then, Kellie just whispered she's going to put some sample first chapters of other series at the back of this book. If you haven't read her Sun Valley Series or her Pacific Bay Series, now would be a great time!

Before saying goodbye, let me urge you to consider a trip to Maui. Don't you dare visit the island without checking out the marina in Lahaina. I'm booking trips daily on the Canefire. Just look for me at the water's edge beyond the Banyan Tree. If you're up for it, we can head over to the Dirty Monkey for a little glass of hooch!

Aloha!

SAMPLE CHAPTER - SISTERS

Chapter 1

Karyn Macadam slowed her car as the sign to the Hemingway Memorial came into view. She turned off Sun Valley Road into the parking area, not bothering to signal. There was no need, not at this early hour.

Cutting the engine, she sat quietly for a few moments, the radio blaring in the background.

And we expect another warm summer day here in the Wood River Valley as residents in this popular resort area prepare to commemorate one of its own, nearly a year and a half after the tragic accident that took the life of—

Karyn shut off the radio, her heart thudding painfully.

Squeezing the steering wheel, she refused to look at the seat next to her—at the small wooden box intricately carved with falling snowflakes over a set of crossed skis.

Deep breath in. Deep breath out.

Five more minutes she sat there, putting off what was ahead.

Finally, she scooped the box into her hands and climbed out of the car.

She'd made a promise. One she fully intended to keep, even if she'd made it a bit tongue-in-cheek at the time.

Gravel crunched beneath her feet as she traversed the walkway toward the memorial. Even in the faint morning light she could make out wild poppies and blue flax, delicate against the pungent skunk cabbage jutting from the pebbled ground lining the trail.

The sound of water bubbling across a rocky streambed pulled her toward the monument nested against a stand of aspen trees, their tiny dollar-shaped leaves barely moving in the still air.

It was understandable why the famous novelist had loved Idaho, why he'd spent his last days living here. Ernest Hemingway was only one of many celebrities who had traded big city tangled traffic for cool mountain mornings and alpine vistas and made Sun Valley their residence.

Olympic hopeful Dean Macadam was another.

Karyn stood at the water's edge and looked past the pile of flat stones with its stately column rising from the middle, beyond the trees to the golf course in the distance. A deer standing in the middle of one of the greens lifted its head and stared back at her in mutual regard.

A voice in her head rang out as clear as if Dean were standing next to her.

"What is your fascination with Hemingway anyway?"

She closed her eyes, remembered gazing up from the pages of *For Whom the Bell Tolls*. "Are you crazy? He was only the best American novelist of all time," she'd so flippantly reminded her husband.

Dean playfully tugged at the sheet tucked around her bare waist. "Is that so?"

She quickly snatched the covering from his hands and

secured it more tightly. "Yes, that's so. In fact, Ernest Hemingway is known for his mastery of theme and imagery. Take this story for example." She held up the heavy volume borrowed from her dad, its cover worn from repeated readings. "The entire narrative is punctuated with a preoccupation with death and dying, which is so poignant given his eventual suicide."

Dean ran broad fingers through his sleep-tousled hair. "Yeah, you see—that's what I don't get. Why is so many people's imagination captured with a guy who spent an inordinate amount of time writing about life instead of living it? I mean, in my view, that's likely what led to him offing himself in the end."

She raised her gaze in horror and slammed the book against her new husband's chest. "Don't say that."

He laughed. "Okay, okay—look, I get it. Ernest Hemingway is your book boyfriend. I'm not jealous. Really I'm not." His eyes nearly sparkled when he'd said that. "Tell you what. When I die, you just take my ashes and toss them in that little creek that runs in front of his memorial. That way, when I'm gone, you can visit both of us at the same time."

Before she could protest the macabre suggestion, he pulled the novel from her and tossed it to the floor, while at the same time lifting the sheet with his other hand.

She'd giggled as he buried his head against her skin. "Promise me. Even if my mother protests and wants otherwise," he said, in a muffled voice. "Now. Promise. Or, I'll—" His fingers dug into her sides and he tickled, sending her entire torso into a fit of squirming. "Promise," he repeated.

"I promise. I promise," she shouted, laughing uncontrollably.

He immediately stopped tickling. "Okay, that's better." Her new husband looked at her then, his eyes boring into her soul. "And promise you'll always remember I love you."

The sound of his voice still seemed so real, even after all

these months. She sunk to the curved stone bench. Tears collected in her eyes and spilled over, making their way down her cheeks. She fingered the familiar lid on the box.

I'm sorry, Dean. I can't do it.

No matter that she'd gotten out of her bed while it was still dark outside with the best intentions. She still wasn't ready to let him go.

Not now—and maybe never.

***

Grayson Chandler wrangled his way past a bunch of willow branches, taking care not to break his fly rod, then headed south crossing into a clearing.

That's when he saw her.

Early thirties. Coffee-colored long hair. Sitting quietly on the stone bench at the Hemingway Memorial.

Not really understanding why, he quieted his steps as he approached.

She held something in her hands, a little box. Her head was tucked. Was she—?

Holding his breath, he moved closer.

Yes, she was crying.

He crouched behind a clump of thick brush and watched, knowing he was encroaching, but unable to help himself.

She was a pretty gal. Frankly, she reminded him a whole lot of that royal lady in England. What was her name? Not Princess Diana, but her son's wife.

Unable to remember, he shook his head. Didn't matter.

What mattered was that she was openly weeping now.

He wavered. Should he step forward? Offer her assistance? He shook his head. Naw—probably not. It wasn't like he carried a handkerchief in his pocket like his dad used to. Likely she just needed some time to get whatever was bothering her out of her system. Women were like that.

Still, he couldn't help but think whatever she was spilling

about was not the least bit inconsequential. Clearly, she was torn up.

Ignoring the reprimanding voice inside that warned him he was being voyeuristic, he rested his fly pole on the ground and continued to watch.

Even crying, she was beautiful, what with her thick lashes sweeping across ivory cheeks that looked as soft as a rose petal. He knotted his hand and pressed it against his lips, imagining brushing his thumb across her skin.

He hadn't thought about a woman in that way for a really long time. Not since—well, since Robin. A subject he didn't care to think about.

The woman on the bench wiped her face with the back of her hand and looked up toward the sky. A few seconds later, she fingered the top of the little wooden box in her lap, chewing at her lip.

Finally, she stood and gazed into the trees, tears still rimming her lashes.

He battled a surge of protectiveness, yet remained still. Under different circumstances he might take a chance, go introduce himself. But he knew better this time.

She turned and saw him. Frowning, she pulled the little box close to her chest.

Face flushed, he reached for his pole and stood. "Hey, I'm sorry. I didn't mean to—what I meant is, I just didn't want to interrupt—" He shook his head. "Look, I'm sorry."

Judging from the way she fidgeted, she too was embarrassed. She tucked a strand of hair behind her ear. "I—I thought I was alone."

"I wasn't really watching. I was doing a little fly fishing." He pointed back at the creek. "I saw you and—"

She rubbed at the place between her eyebrows, then dropped her hand. "Look, I really need to go." She turned and starting walking toward the parking lot.

He wanted to say something more, maybe get her name, but thought better of it.

Upon reaching her car, she glanced back.

In an awkward attempt to apologize again for his intrusion on her private moments, he nodded and gave her a faint smile.

Inside, he wanted to kick himself.

WANT TO READ MORE?

Download here:

www.kelliecoatesgilbert.com/books/sisters

SAMPLE CHAPTER - CHANCES ARE

Chapter 1

Allie Barrett's hands gripped the steering wheel a little tighter as her car headlights lit up the winding two-lane blacktop lined with ferns and canopied by spruce. She rolled down her window. Instantly, the air inside her 1998 Chevy Blazer filled with the scent of pine and salt air, signaling she must be nearing the coast.

She glanced in the rearview mirror at the sleeping boy in the back seat and smiled. Her son needed the sleep. It'd been a long trip.

Ahead, a sign appeared alongside the road saying she had less than a hundred miles to her destination. Feeling a mixture of anticipation and nerves, she fiddled with the radio knob. Unable to tune into a station that didn't crackle, she finally gave up and hummed a favorite Taylor Swift tune about starting over, her new life theme.

She held that thought as doubts sprouted, hoping she hadn't made the wrong decision. She couldn't start a new life if she kept trying to hold onto the old one. Did she want to live a half of a life?

No—she wanted the whole shebang. Even if this move was scary.

With her full attention directed on the road, she rounded a tight bend and squinted against the darkness. The car engine made a knocking noise as the road headed into a sharp incline. Allie pressed the gas pedal down and hoped for the best. The last thing she needed was car trouble.

Her old Chevy Blazer had made it over the past three thousand plus miles without incident, a real feat for a vehicle with over one hundred and fifty thousand miles on its odometer and a paint job that had seen much better days.

Until this past week, she'd never ventured out of Texas. Few would have imagined she'd have the guts to pack up Ryan and head to Oregon, least of all her ex-husband—bless his wandering heart.

It hadn't been easy, living as a single mother. While she'd been on her own for most of their marriage, living without Deacon Ray was still an adjustment, even after nearly two years. She often felt like an armadillo waddling the side of the road about to get smashed by a wayward tire.

So, when that letter arrived from Oregon . . . Well, the way she figured it, that letter was the hand of God presenting her with the opportunity to start over, a chance to create a new life for Ryan and herself. Oh sure, a surprise inheritance was like a plot out of those romance novels her mama used to read, but she didn't care. She'd take it.

She desperately needed a new life.

Allie had never met her benefactor, but her mama spoke of her uncle often. She was so proud of her little brother and all he'd built. "He has a fishing boat out there, Allie. Made it big for a kid from Ding Dong."

Yes, there really was a town in Texas called Ding Dong.

Her hometown, located about an hour north of Austin, was founded in the 1930s by a couple named Zelis and Burt Bell, who owned a store in town. One day, they hired a painter to paint their store sign. A local jokester convinced the painter to paint two bells on the sign and label them Zelis and Burt after the couple, and then write under the bells, "Ding Dong." The painter took the advice and the town was known as Ding Dong ever since.

Today, the tee-niny town had dwindled to near non-existence—only had a couple dozen homes, a café on Main Street, one tiny Southern Baptist church where her daddy used to pastor and a volunteer fire department made up of three old men well into their retirement. Men who could barely lift a firehose, let alone climb a ladder.

Truth was, she hadn't been back to Ding Dong in ages. Not since moving to Dallas with Deacon Ray the year after Mama died. At the time, she'd been pregnant and filled with hope. Of course, that hadn't all turned out as she'd wanted.

At the hillcrest, a deer stood motionless and alert in a clearing alongside the road, a little fawn by her side. As the headlights neared, the doe and its baby bolted into a thick stand of pines.

She glanced at her watch. Two o'clock a.m. Her destination was still over an hour away.

Perhaps she should have stayed in Portland for the night, but her meager budget wouldn't allow for the cost of an extra night in a hotel. While the drive south on Interstate 5 had been an easy drive, she hadn't counted on how this leg of I-20 heading west to the coast, with its long and winding roadway through the Cascade mountain range, would slow her progress.

A loud pop rang out, followed by a raucous *thapping* sound as rubber slapped against pavement.

Allie groaned out loud and gripped the steering wheel tightly to keep the car from veering off-road.

A flat tire—that's all she needed!

Ryan's head bolted up from the backseat. "Mom?" He rubbed at his eyes. "What's that noise?"

"Shhh...go back to sleep, baby. It's just a flat tire. I'll have it fixed in no time. Really, lie down and go back to sleep."

"But you might need help—"

"No, baby. I got it. Go back to sleep." Allie eased the vehicle onto a wide spot in the road and pulled to a stop, turned on her emergency flashers.

She sighed as she glanced out the window at the steep hillside covered with thick pine trees. She'd lost cell service miles back.

Undeterred, she reached over the front seat to the glove box and pulled out a flashlight and a pair of gloves before she stepped into the pitch-black darkness. It'd been over an hour since she'd seen another car, which wasn't necessarily a bad thing. The scene outside would have made the perfect setting for a slasher movie.

Before her mind could take off in wild places, Allie stubbornly yanked the gloves onto her hands and used the dim flashlight to make her way to the back of the car. The tire was a goner.

After surveying the damage, she carefully pulled open the rear hatch door.

Straddling the trailer hitch to the U-Haul, Allie unloaded the tightly packed contents from the Blazer's rear compartment onto the road so she could gain access to where the spare was stored.

A bank of fog broke overhead. Moonlight shone through the misty forest providing much-needed light for the task ahead. She pulled the dusty tire from the cargo area and dropped it onto the loamy soil lining the pavement. The tire bounced a couple of times before falling on its side, making a circling motion and finally coming to a rest.

Well, let's see if I remember how to do this.

Allie brushed the dirt from her gloved hands and reached for the jack kit. She laid the tools onto the pavement and said a little prayer as she kicked the spare tire forward and dropped down on one knee to loosen the lug nuts on the rim, remembering when she and her mama had a flat tire on their way to church years ago.

"C'mon, Allie girl. We've got a tire to fix," her mama said, climbing out of their old Pontiac.

"Why don't we go knock on Mr. Pearson's door and see if he'll help us?"

Her mama shook her head vehemently. "The good Lord helps those who help themselves. Besides, a twelve-year-old should know how to change a tire. Now get on over here close and I'll show you how."

Allie smiled at the memory as she reached for the tire iron. Once she'd popped off the hub cap, she picked up the lug wrench and attempted to loosen the lug nuts. Unfortunately, they wouldn't budge.

A sound interrupted the darkness. Her skin prickled. It was the sound of someone—or something—walking across broken branches.

She swallowed.

Probably another deer, she told herself as she forced her way to a large stone at the edge of the road, determined not to let silly fear get the better of her. She wedged the flashlight between her armpit and forearm, then leaned and picked the heavy rock up before nervously glancing around at the shadows satisfied the large stone had two uses, if necessary.

She lugged the rock back to the car and used the bulky heft to knock against the dangling lug wrench. Once—bam! Twice—bam!

Third time's a charm.

Allie held her breath and slammed the rock harder this

time. She felt the lug give way. She exhaled, feeling immense relief. "That should do it."

Minutes later, she had the tire replaced and the flat stored back in place. Satisfied, she went to work and repacked their belongings, including a nearly empty cooler she'd filled with food so they didn't have to stop and spend money on the trip.

In a moment of weakness, she'd given in to Ryan's pleas for a treat and pulled in to a Burgerville drive-in while driving through Portland. They splurged on an order of big ole Walla Walla sweet onion rings and a shared milkshake, even though that hazelnut shake cost a whopping four dollars.

Her stomach growled. That stop had been hours ago.

Putting mind over matter, Allie stifled a yawn and slid back into the front seat of her car where the deed to her recently deceased uncle's house and title to his fishing boat were tucked securely inside her bag, right next to her divorce papers.

Allie tried like crazy to hold on to her marriage, but there were just so many times she could forgive after coming home to find some girl in her bed. A gal had her dignity, you know?

Those two years since their split had been hard ones, especially for Ryan. As time went on, his dad reached out less and less. Despite shared custody, he seemed to always have excuses for why he couldn't keep Ryan for the weekend or his holidays.

Then Deacon Ray got a wild hair and took off out-of-state for a job months ago. She'd heard through the grapevine he had a gal with him. Except for a Christmas card months ago, they hadn't heard from him since.

She checked the backseat. Despite all the noise she'd been making, Ryan was still sound asleep.

That was the most difficult thing in all of this—trying to help her little boy understand how life could be sometimes.

But, like her mama always said, "When things take a turn for the worse, simply flip the page. Chances are, you never know what story might be in the very next chapter."

She breathed in deeply, let the heady smell of that Oregon air coming in from the open car window clear her head.

She was doing exactly that—stepping into the next chapter. There were lots of reasons to be apprehensive, but life could still deliver a happily ever after ending.

Feeling more than ready to get back on the road, she eased the car back onto the narrow two-lane highway.

Fighting to stay awake, Allie drove the final miles of her long journey in silence until she rounded a wide bend in the road where a large sign lit by floodlights at the base came into view. A lighthouse and a whale were carved in the middle with large gold lettering that read: *Welcome to Pacific Bay. Oregon's friendliest town.*

A buzzy feeling ran down her back. With a trace of a smile, she gripped the steering wheel and focused on the town that lay ahead, relishing the faint apricot-colored morning dawning over the misty rooftops.

This was their new chapter. She couldn't wait for the story to unfold.

WANT TO READ MORE?
Download here:
www.kelliecoatesgilbert.com/books/chances-are

ACKNOWLEDGMENTS

A special word of thanks to the folks at Maui Pineapple Plantation (waving to Debbie, Lacey, Mary and Ken!) These fine people let me hang with them and see how pineapples are planted, grown and harvested.

Did you know pineapple crowns are planted in the earth by hand? The pineapples take fourteen to fifteen months to grow. Maui is known for wild pigs and if they break through the fencing, they can eat a football field worth of produce in no time.

The Maui Pineapples are picked to order and are the sweetest treat you'll ever pop in your mouth...no, really! I had such a fun time on the tour and learned so much. You guys were so supportive of this series and my heart is filled with gratitude.

Thanks also to Elizabeth Mackay for the fabulous cover designs, to Jones House Creative for my web design, to my editors, proofreaders, and my publishing team, including the fabulous Cindy Jackson. Special thanks to my personal assistant, Danielle Woods. You guys all make this business so much easier, and definitely more fun.

To all the readers who hang with me at My Book Friends and She's Reading, you are a blast! I can't believe how much fun it is to do those live author chats and introduce you to my author buddies.

Finally, to all my readers. All this is for you!

~ Kellie

ABOUT THE AUTHOR

USA Today Bestselling Author Kellie Coates Gilbert has won readers' hearts with her compelling and highly emotional stories about women and the relationships that define their lives. A former legal investigator, she is especially known for keeping readers turning pages and creating nuanced characters who seem real.

In addition to garnering hundreds of five-star reviews, Kellie has been described by RT Book Reviews as a "deft, crisp storyteller." Her books were featured as Barnes & Noble Top Shelf Picks and were included on Library Journal's Best Book List.

Born and raised near Sun Valley, Idaho, Kellie now lives with her husband of over thirty-five years in Dallas, where she spends most days by her pool drinking sweet tea and writing the stories of her heart.

For a complete listing of books and to connect with Kellie, visit her website:

www.kelliecoatesgilbert.com

ALSO BY KELLIE COATES GILBERT

Otherwise Engaged

All Fore Love

-

TEXAS GOLD SERIES

A Woman of Fortune

Where Rivers Part

A Reason to Stay

What Matters Most

-

STAND ALONE NOVELS

Mother of Pearl

* * *

Available at all retailers

www.kelliecoatesgilbert.com

Made in the USA
Monee, IL
12 April 2025